AF270883

THE LAST REAL GIRL

L.C. WARMAN

greenleaf &
plympton

Copyright © 2019 by L.C. Warman

All rights reserved.

To respect the copyright of this work, please do not reproduce any part of this book in any form or by any electronic or mechanical means, including information storage and retrieval systems, without written permission from the author, except for the use of brief quotations in a book review.

This book is a work of fiction. Any similarity to actual events or persons, living or dead, is coincidental.

Address:
Greenleaf & Plympton
P.O. Box 36621
18640 Mack Ave.
Grosse Pointe Farms, MI 48236-9998

Greenleaf & Plympton is a publisher of gothic books, both classic and modern. To see our full catalog, visit www.greenleafandplympton.com.

Cover art: Caroline Teagle Johnson

Proofreading: Alexandra Ott

Library of Congress Control Number: 2019931171

ISBN (e-book) 978-1-950103-00-3

ISBN (print) 978-1-950103-01-0

CONTENTS

THE LAST REAL GIRL

*B*reathtaking—that was the word they used to describe her, before and after she went missing. Charlotte Walters wasn't one of those girls that you idealized in retrospect; she was stunning, smart, charismatic, everything and anything that a seventeen-year-old wished to be. And then one day, she was gone.

That was in October. The cold had come early that year. Frost crept up the windows of our cars during the night, kissed the telephone poles at school and danced across the windows that gave melancholic views of the lake, which would soon crust over with its own layer of ice. Everything was slowing down, stiffening, draining of life. College applications were being sent in a frenzy; early admissions decisions were only six weeks away, the date ominous and foreboding. Halloween decorations had been scattered across the school, but there was something nightmarish and gaudy about them this year. They seemed, all at once, a little too real.

"Let's have a Halloween party," Charlotte said to me

one day at lunch, when we had slipped out of the school to skip the whole food thing and drive for a coffee—more specifically, a pumpkin eggnog latte—which was Charlotte's latest form of dieting. She didn't need to; of course she didn't need to. She was always toothpick thin, but with just the right curves, and the delicate bone structure that gave her wrists and ankles the look of something frail and delicate and otherworldly, like a bird's. When I first met her, I used to obsess about the way she brought her long, thin hands to her teeth, chewing at the nails, fluttering like something trying to take flight. Later those nights, I would look at my own wrists, solid and flat and practical. I would try to move my hands like Charlotte's, but they only twitched like heavy spiders. I had wavy blonde hair to Charlotte's dark brown, freckled skin to her olive tones, brown eyes to Charlotte's brilliant, shocking blue. Not even our wrists, I concluded, could be alike.

"A Halloween party," I repeated, because I knew that Charlotte was not asking.

"Yes. At my house. My parents will be gone this weekend."

"What about your brother?"

"What about him? He's at state." She flicked her gaze at me, manicured fingernails drumming on the steering wheel. Most weekends this year, Aiden Walters had returned home from state, where he should have been partying and puking and altogether living up his freshman year, his first year of real freedom. Charlotte had only said, with a roll of her eyes, that he was "homesick," but I had felt the heavy atmosphere of confusion, of *wrongness*, whenever I visited Charlotte on those weekends. Charlotte's parents wore smiles even more forced than normal, and Aiden always slipped away from me. If we went to sit in the living room to watch TV, he would pick up his text-books without a word and drift to another part of the Walters' lakeside house.

I knew better than to press further. I assumed that she had taken care of it, because Charlotte took care of everything.

"Field hockey?" I said.

"No games. States are next week. Geez, Reese, it's like you're trying to find a reason we can't have one." Her tone was angry, but she flashed me a quick smile as we pulled into the drive thru. Charlotte ordered for both of us, two medium pumpkin eggnog lattes with whip.

"So anyway," she said, holding out her credit card to the gawking barista at the window. It was her turn to pay, a wordless rhythm that we never needed to discuss, that we fell into effortlessly. "We need decorations. Food. Booze, obviously. I think Perry will help with that."

"Maybe we can make a trip Friday to Giordano's. They have decorations and pumpkins outside. And Halloween-themed food."

"Excellent." She handed me my pumpkin latte, and a whiff of sharp cinnamon and nutmeg struck me. "Let's start working on the invite list. Party will be Saturday, at eight. So basically everyone will start showing up around nine."

"Right."

We drove back towards school, sipping on our lattes, blasting the heat our way as we rubbed cold, whitened hands on our legs to warm them up. Charlotte stretched hers in front of the air vents, cursing the chill. She said she'd probably freeze to death if she was outside longer than an hour. An image flashed into my mind, a Charlotte with pale skin and blue lips, frost crystals at the corners of her eyes. In my mind she was a frozen fay, her movements slow but still elegant, her blue eyes even sharper, wider. I shook my head.

"Oh, and Reese?" Charlotte said, as we pulled back into the school parking lot. "Don't mention anything to Mindy. About the party."

Mindy. Charlotte's co-captain on the field hockey team. The person who really should have been Charlotte's best friend, if she weren't so loyal to me. Mindy: pretty, athletic, and with a signed letter of intent to play at Dartmouth next year, because athletes and Ivy Leagues could do things their own way, not play the game of admissions letters and bureaucratic waiting.

I didn't ask why. I thought later about what would have happened if I did, if it would have changed something. Changed everything.

Instead, I just nodded.

CHAPTER 2

The first thing you have to understand is that nothing about Charlotte was ordinary. She had a 4.0 grade point average, had been named to the All-State team junior year, and had a talent for painting that made our art teacher, Mr. Pyrtle, cry out that Charlotte MUST pursue a career in the arts, she just MUST.

Nobody had ever told me that I needed to pursue a career in anything. But people were always trying to guide Charlotte, because Charlotte was just so full of *potential*. She could do anything, become anyone. People saw her and projected all of their dreams onto her, because she seemed like a girl who could achieve them. She would laugh about this later, pull faces to mimic those hungry voices. But I think it saddened her, a little.

That's not to say she was perfect. She wasn't going to be our valedictorian. She had taken the SAT and the ACT three times, because her parents were disappointed with her initial scores and didn't know that she had skipped her prep sessions to make out with Rex, one of the captains of the football team. She couldn't sing a tune, and she was a poor swimmer. In our mandatory P.E. class, she had in fact faked cramps for three months straight and flunked out (a doctor's note had later taken care of that). But these were minor little flaws, like salt in a sweet dish, that only brought out how utterly perfect Charlotte otherwise was.

And—yes, it was a cliché—it was hard to say no to her. Charlotte told you that she wanted something, and you moved heaven and earth to get it for her. So when she told me that Friday that she wanted a keg, a proper college keg, for the party, I promised that I would take care of it.

It took all of a couple of hours for me to realize my mistake. Charlotte could have texted any one of a dozen boys, and they would have made the same promise, except they would have *known* how to procure one. I was forced to start texting the few people whose numbers I had, begging for the same favor, with none of the charisma. At lunch, my palms were sweaty as I waited for Charlotte outside, trying to figure out if I dared to use social media to ask some other boys—who usually wouldn't spend much time talking to me, unless Charlotte were close by—if they would do this for her.

"You good?"

I jumped as a hand landed on my shoulder. I had a sudden flashing fancy of a giant scorpion, scuttling across my skin, reaching dark pincers for my neck, before the image dissipated and a pale, freckled hand withdrew. Riley. I exhaled.

"Sorry," Riley said, throwing his hands up in the air in mock surrender. His pug nose scrunched up into his face as he grinned. "You looked spooked. Guess I didn't help."

"Do you know where to get a keg?"

Riley's eyebrows shot up. I didn't care. I was desperate, at this point. Only one person had texted me back thus far, with the insulting and cutting, *Who is this?* Guess saving the sidekick's number just wasn't as important.

But Riley. Riley could do. He would have to. "Please," I said. "It's important. For a party."

I felt him studying me and blushed. I used to tutor Riley in math, back in freshman year. It was a school program, and I needed the volunteer credits. Didn't make it any less mortifying to tutor someone my own age, a hockey player, no less, who had a quick tongue and that easy air of someone completely at home in themselves. I had had a secret, pining crush on him for three full weeks until he made out with Mindy at a party, something his friends teased him about at the learning center during our session. They had dated for two months after that, and by the time it was done I had found enough not to like about him: that rounded pug nose that I had first found cute; the way his eyes wandered when I tried to talk to him about math, looking instead for the next joke to tell or prank to pull; the height that was only an inch or two more than mine; and finally, finally, that even though he waved to me in the hall and said hi in front of his friends, he never straightened up or preened the way he did when he saw a girl like Charlotte pass by.

One day, I thought, I'd find someone who preferred me to Charlotte.

But right now I didn't need a boyfriend or a declaration of undying, Charlotte-free love. I needed a keg.

"A party," Riley repeated. I noticed he had a math

worksheet clutched in one hand—the real reason he had approached me. "This Charlotte's Halloween party?"

"Yes."

"Am I invited? Don't worry," he said, as I visibly tensed. "We already got the invites."

"We?"

"Hockey team." He grinned. "You need to relax more."

I hated it when people told me that. "So can you help?"

"Yeah, I can help. Now?"

I clapped my hands together before my brain could catch up and prevent such idiocy. "Oh, thank you," I said, and just managed to prevent myself from reaching out to hug him. "Really, thank you. Tomorrow at noon? We can bring it to Charlotte's house beforehand."

"I'll just bring it when we come, sound good?"

"Oh—oh, sure. I'll get you the money tomorrow." My hands flapped around my wallet, but I knew I didn't have the cash on me. Besides, how much did a keg cost anyway? Twenty dollars? Forty dollars?

"Great. Hey, could I bother you to take a look at this?"

It was as I leaned over Riley's math assignment that the thought crept to me, slow and needling: if Charlotte had asked him, he would have pretended to need her the whole day. He'd have driven her around looking at all sorts of kegs, just to spend some more time with her. With girls like Charlotte, boys squeezed every drop they could. With me, it was all business, all transaction.

A car horn honked. "Here," I said, snatching the pen from Riley's hand as I glanced up at Charlotte, who was tossing back her hair as she adjusted her rearview mirror. She gave the car another honk for good measure, and someone behind her in the traffic circle answered with one of their own. She flipped them off and waved again at me.

I wrote out the math problem in a hurried scribble for Riley. "You can do the rest that way," I said. "You have to factor the terms—here, and here. You see?"

But Riley was staring at Charlotte. Of course he was. He took the pen and paper from me absentmindedly.

"Do you want to go to the party?" Riley asked, as I swung my bag over my shoulder.

"What?"

Riley shook himself, as if coming to. "Nothing," he murmured. He gave me a quick grin as Charlotte laid on the horn again. "Just thought someone like you would prefer math homework to a party."

"Sorry to disappoint, but I'll be there," I said. It had meant to come out joking and light, to match his tone, but there was a little too much realness to it. It poured from my mouth bitter and hot, and Riley blinked up at me, his expression changing. Mortified, I spun around and hopped in the car, cheeks burning.

"How's our favorite albino mountain troll?" Charlotte said, zipping out onto the road.

"He's bringing a keg tomorrow."

"Oh, lovely! My savior. Hey," she said, as she braked hard at the red light, sending us careening forward against our seatbelts. "You know what's spooky? Ghosts. Like Cassandra Lewis."

I glanced sideways at Charlotte. Cassandra Lewis was a thick, gorilla-looking girl with a bad unibrow and a slow, pitiful gaze. She had disappeared a few months ago from school, and Charlotte had been one of the only people to notice. Charlotte was like that; she paid attention even when you thought she wasn't. Most people figured Cassandra's parents had sent her to boarding school, or else switched to homeschooling, but Charlotte had insisted on going by the house to find out. I had looked up the address in the directory with her. Turned out the parents had clean moved out, which disappointed Charlotte; it meant that Cassandra had likely moved, and not been kidnapped or murdered or abducted by aliens, as would make the better story.

"They still might have left out of grief," Charlotte had said hopefully, and I had murmured some form of agreement.

But now I only waited as Charlotte drove on, humming slightly to herself, looking mischievous and a little pleased. "The theme," Charlotte announced, as she took a sharp curve onto a side road, "will be ghosts. Ghosts of dead girls, in fact."

"Is that a theme?"

"Of course it's a theme."

"Okay, so… You want me to bring some extra bedsheets?"

Charlotte laughed, throwing her head back so far that I almost wanted to grab the wheel from her. "You wait and see," she said. "My place at three tomorrow. You're going to help me bake cookies."

"Ghost-shaped, I hope?"

Charlotte grinned. But just as quickly it faded. The shadows on her face, mottled and shifting as the sun broke through the passing leaves, looked like writhing snakes on her skin.

The silence lasted for one minute, then another. Charlotte looked serious, and the suddenness of the change threw me.

"Reese," she said finally, voice low, "do you sometimes think there's something *wrong* with St. Clair?"

"St. Clair?" I said, the name of our town sweet and sharp like a bell in my mouth. St. Clair was beautiful. Picturesque. A kid like Charlotte probably took it for granted, idealized it, hated it because someone with money could. Could actually think that they might escape to a big city one day, away from the suburban glamor and old-money confidence of a place like our lakeside town. Could laugh away the four or five or nine generations of Walters who had lived there before her, because they were like stone weights around her neck, because she didn't know what it was like to come to St. Clair at eleven and be forced to live among a set of students who took for granted that your parents were together, that they vacationed in Aspen, that they looked down with cloying suffocation on anyone who lived "beyond the hill."

"Sometimes," Charlotte said, "I think we're all a little crazy here."

I responded with a noise that might have been either assent or dissent.

"Except for you," Charlotte said. "You're not. Not yet."

CHAPTER 3

*W*e spent most of that day shopping and decorating; Charlotte had field hockey practice Saturday morning, and so I was tasked with picking up some of the harder-to-find items that we had missed Friday. I used my mom's car to putter first to the market, and then to the Halloween store, the latter surrounded by an explosion of pumpkins and white cobweb fuzz that made it hard to walk without getting entangled in something.

And then noon came, and I was out of things to do, and I had missed two calls from my mother already. I considered going to a coffee shop and sitting down with a maple latte, perhaps doing a little bit of the homework I had in my backpack. But no; my mother's hospital shift started soon, and as much as we argued and fought for control of the car, I wasn't stupid or selfish enough to think that my joyriding came before her work.

I timed my arrival late enough that my mother had only the opportunity to deliver a few sharp words before she took the keys and reversed out of the driveway. I watched her go, her thick wavy hair plaited in a severe braid down her back, her freckled skin bagged and wrinkled from the stress of her job, from me, from the unforgiving winters in St. Clair. I wondered for a moment if she still told people she was from Florida; I had stopped doing so years ago, when I felt that the land of crabgrass and sunshine no longer had a tight hold on me. But I suppose for her, it would always be home. St. Clair was exile.

I lugged in my bags and fended off the whining, excited overtures from Morty, our shepherd rescue. He bounced left and right and forward and back as I deposited the bags on the counter, chasing his white tail, then coming to a low crouch, then bounding across the room and leaping up onto our green sofa. "I know," I said. "Groceries are quite exciting."

Morty barked his agreement.

My mother had never really told me why we had to move, all those years ago. I tried to picture it as I packed up the decorations and moved some perishables into the fridge. I had come home from school one day, sticky and warm from the sun, and she had sat me down with a lopsided smile. "Guess what, darling?" she had said. "We're moving north!"

"To Jacksonville?" I said. My mother had friends there; she'd often talk wistfully about it.

"Jacksonville? Oh, no! No, darling, much further. Right near Canada, actually."

At this point, my mother used to tell me, I broke down and started crying, saying I didn't want to be Canadian. That's not how I remember it: I remember talking quite calmly about whether we were to become Canadians, and learning that no, we would be moving to a lakeside town on the outskirts of a city, with a great hospital program for my mother. I think she had talked then of more schooling, of a degree program or specialized training of some sort, but if that's why we moved it never panned out; my mother had the same job she always did, tough but reliable, demanding but impressive. And a few months in, she began dating Jerry, a local tax accountant, who left her for a hairdresser three years later and then moved her and his two apple-faced children to Denver.

I thought about Charlotte's question the night before: *Do you think there's something* wrong *with St. Clair?* If there was, I couldn't see it, at least not on the surface. The entire place was out of a storybook. Most of the city was grids of manicured houses with freshly cut lawns and medians, perfectly square sidewalks and oak and maple trees lining the wide streets. The houses were all brick or white stone, with wrought-iron gates and little detached garages. And that was only on the regular side of town—go east, towards the water, and the flat idyllic land and cute little downtown transformed into rolling hills and wooded roads, like you were entering some kind of fairy tale. It was here where the rich of the rich lived, in castle-like houses on the shore, overlooking the wide and dark lake. It was here where Charlotte's family lived, in a house fit for royalty, with a driveway half a mile long and a balcony off the master where we'd have coffee and whiskey the mornings when Mr. and Mrs. Walters were gone, kicking our feet through the stone balustrades and talking about tales of kids who had once tried to swim across the lake.

I shook myself and looked at the clock. Still another two hours to kill. I pulled out my homework, made some instant coffee, and plunged onto the sofa, where Morty hopped up and immediately rested his chestnut head on my thigh. I petted him absently. My pen hovered over my trig problems, and my eyes darted between our warped floors, our cracked fireplace, and the perpetually dew-covered windows of our little townhouse. It was a nice place to live; I knew it was, I was grateful for it, and my mother certainly reminded me of our landlord's kindness in keeping rent stable all these years (they were both single mothers, and at various times I had to be subjected to awkward dinners with Mrs. Leaventrott, who would wear pearls and a patterned flower dress and size me up with her cataract-clouded eyes, trying to decide if I was the type of girl who deserved her continued charity).

But our home was nothing compared to Charlotte's—and I'm not talking about the rent vs. own divide. I knew I shouldn't be jealous. I knew that envy could be ugly, caustic, eating up your insides with its insidious whispers of how much you deserved and how little everyone else did. But my jealousy was of a different nature. I did not begrudge Charlotte her wonders. I was amazed that she had chosen to share them with me.

The story was always so fascinating to people, but the truth was, it was simple: Charlotte was rich and pretty and charismatic. At a certain point in middle school, her friends turned against her. And then I came to town: a blank slate, a fresh start. Charlotte cleaved to me. Even when the girls came around, even when they wanted her back, Charlotte never abandoned our friendship. She knew she could trust me more than all of those girls put together, and we were best friends the moment she sat down at my empty table in middle school, offered me half of a peanut butter sandwich, and said, "I need new friends. Are you interested?"

I was.

WHEN I ARRIVED at Charlotte's a little past three, she shouted down the wide stair banister in the two-floor entryway that she would be down in a few minutes. "Face mask!" she shouted, by way of explanation, before the door slammed shut.

I moved to the kitchen and began unloading supplies. Charlotte already had the ghost cookie cutters laid out for us to use; I found myself amused and then a little excited at the ridiculousness of the theme.

I was about to toss the eggs in the fridge when I paused. Taped on the outside of the fridge was a photo of the family. Charlotte's mother, tall and slim and blonde, with Charlotte's striking blue eyes and tilted cheekbones. Charlotte's father, broad-shouldered and beaming, arm draped proudly across the back of his wife and two kids. Charlotte, in a long slip of a black dress, dark hair draped luxuriously across her shoulders, expression sweet but also a little wicked, like she was laughing at you behind the camera. And then her brother, Aiden.

I stepped closer.

His expression was odd. Like the camera had caught him by surprise. His brows were furrowed, his mouth puckered, and his hands were thrust deep into his pockets, as though he wished to disappear. There was something urgent about him. For a moment I imagined him stepping outside of the photograph, pulling his hands out of his pockets to stretch them out towards me. "Listen," he would say, "you have to know—"

"What are you doing?"

I startled. Some of the eggs tumbled from the carton and landed with a sickening *splat* on the hardwood below, gooey yolk oozing across the floorboards. I quickly placed the rest of the carton on the counter and began to flutter about looking for paper towels, my face a burning red. I felt rather than saw Aiden sigh and put down his bag, and tear off a sheet to help me.

"Sorry," he said gruffly, pulling out a spray bottle of lemon floor cleaner from beneath the sink. "I shouldn't have startled you."

I risked a glance up at him. The animosity still had not left his voice. His expression was hardly much friendlier. It was always trippy to look at him; he was the spitting image of Charlotte (I'd forever think of it that way, even though Aiden was a year older). He had the same dark hair, the same bright blue eyes and tilted cheekbones, the same elegant hands. He was more solid though, more real and less fairy, with the broadness of his father and a height about six inches taller than his willowy sister. I knew plenty of girls in our grade who had been obsessed with him, and I was convinced that it was at least half of the reason why, all those years ago, Charlotte had been welcomed back into their good graces. Aiden had been a lacrosse player, and had even had some offers to play D3 in various out-of-state prestigious liberal arts colleges. I didn't know why he had chosen state; I had always assumed that it was because it was the natural choice for almost everyone who could get in. It was most likely where I was going, next year—though that was because I couldn't afford to carry loans from anywhere else.

"Here," I said, taking the dirty paper towels from him as he set to work on the final splooch. I deposited them into the Walters' kitchen trash, in the tub hidden away in a soft-closing cabinet. Aiden rubbed the last spot and straightened, jerking right to throw the rest of the paper towels away.

"I thought you would be gone this weekend," I blurted out, and then blushed as his gaze turned towards me.

I found myself unable to hold the gaze for very long, and instead my eyes flickered over his long-sleeved T-shirt, his polo shorts, his loafers. Was that hate I could feel radiating off of him? Aiden had always been polite but distant towards me, but something had changed since last summer. Something that had made him cool towards everyone, that had made his presence something heavy and uncomfortable, almost awkward. Charlotte wouldn't talk about it, and I couldn't very well ask anyone else what had happened. I supposed he had gotten in trouble, somehow. That his weekends home were penance for some unknown sin.

"I'm here every weekend," Aiden said finally. "It's my house."

"Well, of course, I didn't mean that," I said, flushing again. I forced myself to meet his gaze, even though it only made me turn redder. "I just—well, are you coming to the party?"

"Not if I can help it."

Right, then. "Well, have a good day," I said, turning my shoulders so that I no longer faced him. I put the remainder of eggs in the fridge and began to busy myself again; no need to continue to try to talk to him if that's how he was going to play it. I wondered if he was rude because he thought I was weird for staring at his family portrait. It *was* weird, but then, who wouldn't be curious?

"Have a good time at the party," Aiden said. There was something in his voice, some catch that I couldn't quite make out. "Sorry for startling you." His footsteps retreated across the hardwood, and then up the stairs. I heard a bright "Hello, brother!" and the click of Charlotte's heels on the floor before the fresh-faced Charlotte appeared in front of me and spun around twice, laughing. She had on a T-shirt and plain shorts, and snatched up a long apron.

"Cookie time!" she said, and for a moment she was not seventeen-year-old Charlotte, hauntingly gorgeous, danger-ously cunning, but the Charlotte of middle school, playful and mischievous and full of easy smiles. I caught the apron she tossed towards me and tied it on.

Charlotte chatted easily on about the guest list for the night, which was large enough that it was apparent it would get out of control. She talked about the handful of football players who were blowing up her phone that after-noon, who assumed, like all boys did who were interested in her, that she must have orchestrated the whole event specially for them. She told me the string of gossip she had heard about last night—parties attended, couples formed and dissolved, girls ditched and boys slighted. I knew rationally that she had learned it all over text, that many people in the school felt gossip wasn't real until Charlotte Walters knew about it, but another part of me felt that the source of her knowledge was deeper, more mysterious, that Charlotte Walters knew everything because she *was* the town, or everything that St. Clair liked to think of itself as. I imagined roots growing down from her feet, expanding out beneath the cold earth, poking up in every house, school, and building and glittering in the frost and ice of late October.

"By the way," she said, as we cut the last of the sugar cookies from the dough and arranged it on the sheet, "I hear Riley has a thing for you. Just be careful. You know, those hockey guys." Her hand flicked in some dismissive motion, and I went very still. I didn't know Aiden was behind me until he reached around to grab the filtered water on the counter.

"No one's staying past two," Aiden said, pouring himself a cup. "And I'm not covering for you if the police are called."

Charlotte rolled her eyes and flashed me a smile, which I returned weakly. At the very least, I thought, the interruption had saved me from having to respond to her warning. Riley? No, she had it all wrong. I thought about the way he had looked at her as she had driven up, the way his gaze followed her that afternoon. It wouldn't be the first time someone had pretended to be interested in me to get in Charlotte's good graces; it was short-sighted and stupid, but you really couldn't expect much more out of high school boys.

"The police won't be called. We're a half mile from anyone else. Who's going to make the noise complaint?"

"It's happened before."

Charlotte again waved her hand dismissively. I felt Aiden's gaze light on me again, and I met it, not wanting to be intimidated. He seemed to be considering something. His mouth opened, then closed.

"Take a picture, it will last longer," Charlotte said, and then snickered when Aiden gave her the finger and left.

I wondered what it was that Aiden had wanted to say.

CHAPTER 4

The party was in full swing by eight o'clock; for Charlotte Walters' parties, there was no fashionably late. No one wanted to miss a moment.

Riley had arrived right on time with the keg. I could feel Charlotte watching us as I let him in, and so I was brusquer than normal, business-like. I asked him a few times how much the keg cost, and he demurred politely once, then twice, before telling me. I handed him the cash, all my wages that were to last me this week and next—my next library paycheck would not be until the Friday after.

Riley hesitated when I held out the cash, but Charlotte was nearby, hanging a few cobweb decorations, and so I smacked the money on the counter and pretended to go busy myself elsewhere. Sure enough, a few moments later Riley was asking Charlotte about the theme of the party, and I was forgotten. No matter. Charlotte wouldn't be interested in someone like him, anyway.

I nursed one cup of beer for those first few hours; my mother was like a bloodhound, and I knew that if I had much more she would sniff it out on me and ground me for weeks. She wasn't the kind of mother who served wine at dinner like the Walters, or who let their children drink so long as it was in the house. Once, last year, I had even seen Mrs. Walters hand Charlotte a cigarette, mother and daughter standing on the top balcony, looking out at the lake as they blew matching puffs of smoke into the wind. I had been on my way out after a sleepover, and the image had stayed with me for months; when I closed my eyes, sometimes I could still see it, the two elegant figures draped over the balustrade, elven ghosts that were as wispy as their smoky breaths.

Mindy, Charlotte's field hockey co-captain, ended up coming after all, as of course Charlotte knew that she would. The important thing was that Mindy had not been invited specifically, that she knew she was not technically welcome. I could see it in the stiff way that Mindy entered the house, flanked by her field hockey friends, the way she laughed too loud at the first joke thrown at her, the way she beelined for the blood-red punch with floating rubber spiders and poured herself a portion before emptying a whiskey nip into it.

I was sitting on the couch in the living room, the black leather L-shaped one that faced the fireplace and the giant TV, on which was playing the tail end of one of the state football games. I could smell cigar smoke wafting in from the patio, and when I turned my head and craned it over the patches of kids sitting and leaning against every available surface, I could make out Charlotte talking to Danny, a football player, as Mindy skulked nearby. Charlotte had on a slinking white dress with a slit up the side;

Mindy, in white behind her, looked like some squashed-down version of Charlotte, half a foot shorter and wider, solid. It was odd, because Mindy was a very pretty girl—funny, too, so everyone liked her and she had more than half the class in love with her. But no one could stand next to Charlotte Walters and look good, except, perhaps, another Walters.

"Let's go to the couch," Charlotte said, as Mindy hovered a step closer, presumably to greet Charlotte, to see for herself whether the snub had been intentional. Danny followed Charlotte to a spot near me, and a few juniors immediately cleared out to make room. "Danny, you know Reese? Reese, Danny."

I nodded at him, though we had met twice before, and he smiled and shook my hand before spinning back to Charlotte.

"You know," Charlotte said, getting up and depositing herself between Danny and me, so she could turn her mischievous gaze my way and turn her shoulder away from Danny, "the last owners of this house told us that the property was haunted."

I felt a prickle at the back of my neck. We'd talked about this before, a couple times, mostly when Charlotte was bored. She would ask me if I believed in ghosts, if I thought that a chill in the air meant some other presence was in the room with you, if I thought that creaking doors and flickering lights could mean anything. I played the scoffing skeptic, starkly unwilling to believe any of that hocus pocus, but in truth it creeped me out, and I would always spend the night after with the lamp on next to my bed, falling asleep in the orange glow because otherwise the shadows were too much for me, the whispers and rustles too loud.

"Haunted?" Danny said, miffed at Charlotte's cold shoulder but not ready to give up yet. His curly black hair flopped over his forehead, and he pushed it back with one of those textbook teenage neck jerks to toss it ineffectually —for just a moment—back over his head. "Like hocus pocus?" He wiggled his hands, and Charlotte rolled her eyes.

"Sure, like hocus pocus," she said. She cast a glance at me, inviting me to share in her amusement. But I didn't have the social capital to laugh at someone like Danny, so I only smiled gently and tucked one leg underneath me. "You remember when you were sleeping over that night, Reese, and we heard those clinks in the kitchen?"

"Someone was getting a midnight snack," Danny said. "I do it all the time."

"Oh yeah? What about the fact that we were the only ones in the house that night?" This was not strictly true— Charlotte's mother had been there. But she slept like the dead, and so it might as well have been.

"Well," Danny said, grinning, pleased that he had coaxed Charlotte's attention back his way, "maybe it was just someone passing through." He grew mock sober. "However, if you're worried and would like someone to stay the night, stand watch—"

Charlotte snorted, but she let Danny throw one arm over her shoulder. I felt a few heads near us turn, the whispers start as a potential pairing surfaced. I wanted to tell them not to bother; it wouldn't last. But instead I rested my chin on my knee and looked up at Charlotte, waiting.

"So who died, then?" Danny said, lowering his voice, but not by much. I could feel others listening in. Danny wanted me to go; that was plain. And I'd be more than happy to. I didn't want to play chaperone, didn't want Charlotte to use me to build tension with this new guy, pretending she had to be a good friend (*oh, but she's sitting all alone*) and spend time with me, all because she never intended to give him what he was after.

"An old man," Charlotte said. "And his wife. The people before us said that he probably killed her."

"Doesn't seem like a great way to sell real estate." Riley deposited himself next to me on the couch, offering me an unopened can of beer. I took it, because it was something to do with my hands, and murmured a thanks. Danny gave him a quick look, assessing the threat.

"Well, they told us after we had bought it, naturally," Charlotte said. "My mom reached out about all of the weird sounds, and that's when they told us."

"Too late to back out, I guess," Danny said.

"Oh, all the contracts around here have provisions in them about ghosts. You didn't know that? You're not allowed to cancel a contract, or sue for that matter, because of ghostly activity."

"That can't be true," I protested.

"It is." Riley swirled the beer around in his own can. "My mom's a realtor. Some leftover clause from the eighteenth century, or something."

A realtor? I hadn't known that. I wondered what Riley's dad did, but I didn't want to ask. The question would always come back to me, and I'd have to say that my dad lived out in New Mexico and was a contractor. Only

27

half of it was true, or at least based on truth—the last child support check my mother had gotten had been from New Mexico, but my father had never done a day's hard labor in his life. He was a trust-fund kid who had partied hard, young, and flirted briefly with monogamy when he met my mother before abandoning it, and us, entirely. I had never whined or complained about this, or threatened my mom that I wanted to go live with him, because it was plainly apparent that in him we had a common enemy, someone who had disrupted her life and catapulted mine into existence, and then disappeared after the explosion, to leave us to pick up the pieces.

"Really?" Charlotte said, shaking me out of my reverie. I was glad, because I noticed then that Riley was studying my expression, that I had maybe let a little too much slip. "That's awesome. Has she seen any haunted houses, then?"

"People have claimed it, here and there. She doesn't really believe in that stuff."

"Doesn't matter if you believe it or not, if it's true," Charlotte said, grinning at him. Danny bristled.

"So an old man," he said. "Kind of a boring ghost. What does he do, complain about his bunions all night?"

"And what would an *interesting* ghost be?" Charlotte asked, turning towards him.

Danny grinned. There was something artificial about it, about both of them actually, that threw me. "Ever heard of Screaming Stella? Out on that island in the middle of St. Clair. If you go out at midnight, on a full moon, you can hear her—"

"Oh, *can* you?"

"It's a full moon tonight," Danny teased. Of course it was. He knew that beforehand. Next thing he was going to tell her was that she could only hear it while skinny-dipping in the water. "We could go out, if you don't believe me."

"And Screaming Stella is—?"

"A young girl who was murdered out there. Probably in like, the 50s, or something."

"Ah," Charlotte said, turning with a wink towards me. "Of course. A young, beautiful girl. It always is."

"It always is what?" Danny said.

"Someone young and beautiful. America is OBSESSED with dead girls," Charlotte said. She cut her gaze sideways towards me. "If I died, Reese, would you be obsessed with me?"

I opened my mouth, paused. "Yes" didn't seem right. "No" didn't either. And I didn't have a witty rejoinder ready.

"So this Screaming Stella," Riley said, saving me from a response. "You hear her at what, midnight?"

"Midnight, lakeside," Danny said. I could have sworn for a moment that I saw fear flash across his face, as if he actually believed this stuff. "And this house is close to the lake—it can't be what, more than a quarter of a mile there?"

Charlotte looked down at her drink. There suddenly seemed something off about her, I thought. Her face was a little gray, her expression pinched. She seemed to be shrinking, withdrawing into herself, even as all the eyes of our little group turned upon her. I heard someone behind us loudly suggest a game of spin the bottle, and another searing voice dismiss him. And there was Charlotte, the beating heart of the party, shriveling.

Then she drew her head back up, and the illusion vanished. She was Charlotte again—brave, reckless, beautiful. "What do you think, Reese?" she said, grinning.

I wasn't going to be the party pooper. "I think we should go," I said. "Let's see if there's any truth in it."

Danny and Charlotte exchanged a glance. Again I felt that odd sense that I was the outsider here, that something else was between them that I couldn't touch. And then Charlotte looked away.

In the next couple of days, I'd replay this scene in my head, over and over. Trying to figure out how it could have gone differently—how it could have been stopped.

CHAPTER 5

The three hours until midnight passed in drips and drabs. I kept nursing the same beer that Riley had handed me, floating between groups, refilling cookie platters and punch bowls, directing people to the bathroom and telling others that it was time to go home. Most people knew me as Charlotte's friend, so they didn't argue when I told them, and I wielded the authority rarely enough that most respected it when I did, too.

The faces and people faded in and out that night, in a constant rotation. I'd find myself in a group of field hockey girls, who wanted to know what was going on between Mindy and Charlotte. I'd extricate myself only to stumble into a group of guys who wanted to know if Danny and Charlotte were hooking up, and turn around to find myself in the middle of yet another huddle, where one of the more enterprising members would ask me if we had any weed ("we're willing to pay"). Twice I ran into Riley again, who always seemed to show up close to my shoulder whenever Charlotte was nearby. The second time it happened was half past eleven, and I had had enough of it.

"Just go talk to her," I said to him. "You'll probably get shot down, but it's worse like this."

"What?" he said, brow furrowing. Unlike many of the other kids here, his face had not slackened with alcohol, and his eyes were still bright, alert.

I pointed a thumb towards Charlotte. "Talk to her," I said.

"Why?"

"Because you want to. Because you should, if you like her. It's better to know either way." I was blushing, but the mass of kids in the crowd made the room hot and sticky, and covered, I hoped, my own color.

"Why would you assume that?" Riley said. He looked, of all things, genuinely angry. Or not angry—upset. I couldn't tell. I ran a hand over my face, conscious of having overstepped.

I couldn't see another way out, so I tapped my still half-full beer can. "Refill," I mouthed, and disappeared. My ears were burning. Well, it was true, wasn't it? He could play righteously indignant if he wanted, but it wasn't like he had been texting me today, or trying to talk to me outside of my connection to Charlotte. I wasn't upset about it; I just didn't want to play the game anymore.

I snuck a glance back at Riley; he was still watching me, face drawn, twisted. I looked away again quickly.

"Ghost brigade!" Danny said as I entered the kitchen. He slapped me on the shoulder. "You in?"

"In," I said, grateful for the excuse to leave. When I snuck another glance back at Riley, he was gone.

All in all, five of us gathered at the door—Danny, Charlotte, myself, and a football-cheerleader couple, Eliot and Karuna, who had evidently taken the promise of a walk in the woods as a promise of solitude. Karuna was giggling as we set off, flashlights in hand. Riley had not shown up.

We had gone no further than ten yards from the house when I heard branches snapping behind us. Despite myself, my heart fluttered; I had wanted Riley to come, after all, and thought perhaps I'd get the chance to apologize for embarrassing him. But Charlotte's face fell, and when I turned back, I saw it was not Riley but Aiden who had followed us.

"Where do you think you're going?"

He had on long, dark pajama pants and a pullover. He had obviously been sleeping, or trying to; his hair was tousled, and his face held the puffiness of a recent doze. I could see a cut on his hand where he must have fallen in the brambles behind us. Aiden held no flashlight, no shoes beyond a flimsy pair of sandals.

"Relax, Aiden," Charlotte said. "We're going to the lake to hear Screaming Stella. We'll be right back."

"Hey, man," Danny said. "I'll take good care of her. We're all going together, and no swimming, promise."

Aiden's gaze fastened on me. "It's not a good idea."

I swallowed. He seemed to be expecting me, somehow, to say something. Karuna and Eliot whispered to each other and then peeled off into the darkness, headed back towards the house. "It won't take long," I said finally.

"Seriously?"

"Aiden," Charlotte said. "Just go back to bed—"

"I'm coming."

Charlotte rolled her eyes and caught my gaze, trying to share a smile. But I saw something nervous underneath it, too, something a little panicked. She hadn't expected this; it was ruining her plan, and I had a feeling that this plan extended beyond a midnight lakeside stroll to hear a ghost that she didn't even believe in.

The party set off again, quiet now. The flirtation between Danny and Charlotte ceased immediately, as if smothered. Danny tried once, haphazardly, to throw his arm around Charlotte's shoulders, but he half missed and his hand bounced and trailed off, and Charlotte did nothing to nestle closer to him. He cast an angry glance back at Aiden, as if somehow it had been Aiden's fault. Aiden, for his part, was not even looking at his sister or Danny. He was staring straight ahead, stoic, angry.

"This is stupid," Charlotte said, coming to a halt. We were in the middle of the woods, close enough to still hear the sounds of the party raging behind us, not yet far enough to see the edge of the dark lake that bordered the Walters' property. "Aiden, you're killing the whole mood. Let's just forget it."

Danny seemed relieved, and more than a little willing to skulk back. Plans of a midnight tryst with Charlotte were obviously dashed, and he probably was hoping to get back and drink enough to rekindle his buzz and finish out the party.

"I didn't say anything," Aiden said. "Go. See the 'ghost' if you want to."

"I don't want to anymore."

Aiden crossed his arms. For a moment, Danny and I

caught each other's gaze, the acknowledgment of our mutual status as outsiders, of the uncomfortableness of witnessing the sharpness and deep history of family conflict. Charlotte must have felt it, too, for she forced herself to laugh, high and not very convincing, and tucked her arm around Danny's. *She's scared of him*, I thought, blinking, not quite believing. And then—no, the thought passed. I could see not fear but hatred in Charlotte's gaze. She didn't fear her brother; she despised him for ruining whatever plan she had.

A trickle of fear went down my back. Did I even know what Charlotte was planning?

The darkness was getting to me. I had read a psychological study once that concluded that darkness increased paranoia. It seemed the kind of stupid, simple scientific piece that wasted everyone's time and money to prove something we already knew: that darkness meant predators, danger, the unknown, and of course when we were in it our minds jumped to all sorts of conclusions, tried to suss out all sorts of possibilities, to save us from the inevitable.

"Let's go back inside," I said.

I couldn't hear the party anymore. Was it because my blood was pounding now, loudly in my ears? Or had we stepped into some sunken little circle of the forest, some bewitched part of the night, where we had passed through a portal and been transported away from the St. Clair we knew and into something else entirely?

My breath caught. I forced myself to breathe: inhale, then exhale. I could see Danny fighting the same instinct; he looked poised to run. He caught my eye.

"Reese should go inside," he said, and I found myself

surprised to hear he remembered my name. "She looks a bit pale."

Charlotte and Aiden's gazes turned towards me. I shrunk away a bit, embarrassed, but even that left me feeling woozy and uncertain, and Aiden caught me by the wrist. He pulled me forward, until I regained the center of my balance, and then let go, his hand still hovering near me.

"Come on, then," he said gruffly.

Aiden walked much more closely to me on the way back. It only took about a minute for us to see the house again, and just a couple more to reach the back door. As the light and sounds poured over us, I felt ridiculous for being so scared back there. Danny likewise grew more animated, making jokes about Screaming Stella, about how she probably wasn't out anyway. Charlotte was quiet, thoughtful. But her bad mood seemed to lift almost as soon as we stepped inside the house; she grabbed a bottle of vodka, poured herself a drink, and cheers-ed the nearest guy with a Cheshire-cat smile.

"To the ghosts of dead girls!" she shouted, and downed the drink. She grinned when she saw me standing nearby and pulled me into a tight hug. She smelled of orange liquor and pine needles, and something else, something almost metallic. Her mouth dipped towards my ear. "We're going to have to go now, when he isn't looking," she said. I turned, to follow her gaze, and caught Aiden ascending the stairs. "Quick! *Now.*" And she disappeared outside of the sliding glass door and back into the forest. I waited for half a second, panicked and uncertain, looking around for anyone, even Danny, to help me make sense of it.

She's drunk, I thought.

And then an image flashed into my mind: the lakeshore's dip.

Another image followed, of Charlotte slipping on the rocks of the place we had always called the cliff, even though it was no more than a dozen man-made feet of carved rock, put into the Walters' property to more aptly mimic an ocean shore. There had been a fence there, once, to keep the children from tumbling down to their deaths, but Mrs. Walters had had it removed when Charlotte turned thirteen, because it was an eyesore. How easy would it be for a laughing Charlotte to run out there, vodka breath warming the October night, feet crunching across broken twigs and pepper-colored stones, to glance over her shoulder, searching for me to follow, for us to find evidence of Screaming Stella together, like we were children again, and then…

Heat rushed over me. I was already thirty seconds behind, if not more. And Charlotte was faster than me.

I ducked out into the night after her.

CHAPTER 6

*I*t was worse, so much worse, being out there on my own.

The night pressed down all around me. The house was swallowed up behind me within seconds; when I looked back, I saw only trees, not even the familiar warm lights of the windows. "Charlotte," I whispered, but something made me afraid to cry out any louder. I felt like I would call something, someone, closer to us.

Still I picked my way across the fallen leaves and dead branches of the forest, the one that Charlotte and I had explored in middle school when her mother refused to drop us off in town, and when we were pretending to retreat to do homework instead. We would walk along the water, and Charlotte would ask me questions like, *if you could move anywhere in the world, where would you?* And, *if you could be anyone at all, who would you be?* Questions that didn't have answers but instead longing behind them, so fierce and thrilling and sweet that it seemed that, at the edge of the lake, the world unfolded out before us, revealing something open and vast and promising.

High school had put an end to those walks; we mostly drove now to where we could see and be seen, at one of the downtown cafés or the diner where once, legend went, a waitress had served a senior a beer, which led to so many countless orders that no doubt if it had been true, the waitress had been put right.

All of that was distant now. I slowed my trot to a walk, conscious of the chill in the air. It couldn't have grown so much colder within just a few minutes, could it? But my breath was coming out in warm bursts of steam, and I worried that I was making too much noise, crunching and sighing and creaking. I thought of Screaming Stella and stiffened, sure that I had heard some sort of whine in the wind. Shivering, I tried to peer forward into the darkness, measure the distance to the lakeshore. What if it was me who catapulted over the edge, as Charlotte laughed and swung her legs on the cliff a few yards down?

I picked my way more carefully through the darkness now, heart still pounding, trying to see anything through the rustling skeletal trees that surrounded me. I wasn't even sure that I was going the proper way; it was a straight shot from the house to the shore, but it seemed to be taking me too long, even though I had sprinted the first portion. I knew that I had ducked around trees here and there—what were the chances, in the night, that I had veered off course? That I'd keep walking and walking and walking, and never find the lake?

I looked up through the trees at the pale moon floating overhead. It didn't seem to be much help; I tried to remember where it had been when we had been out here before, the four of us together, but my memory kept tilting and sliding beneath me.

"Charlotte," I said, trying to raise my voice just slightly now, too panicked to keep silent. "Charlotte, if you're out there, come here. It's not funny."

I thought I heard a laugh on the wind. Or was it a shriek? I paused, my blood running cold, straining to hear anything above the cracks and creaks of the forest, afraid that I *would* hear something, would give myself away. After a few seconds of silence, I took one step closer to a tree, pressing my hand into it, trying to feel as though I had at least one point of attack covered, one spot of vulnerability patched up. I wanted to run back, but now I wasn't even sure where back was. My heart pounded.

A splash echoed to my right.

I tore off at once, as eager to get to the noise as to spot the water, to reorient myself in this dark fairy-tale other-world that I had found myself in. I broke across the edge of the cliff seconds later and came to a staggering halt, my heels digging in on the shifting pebbles as I pinwheeled backwards and landed hard on the earth. I scrambled back up and froze in a half crouch.

Someone was in the water.

In a rowboat.

I leaned deeper into the grass, praying that they hadn't heard me. It didn't seem like it. Could be anyone, a voice in my head tried to say. A neighbor, out for a midnight paddle. Some security guard, doing his rounds. That was a thing, right?

But it didn't look like it. The figure was facing towards

the shore, paddling away from it, but a dark hoodie was drawn over its head, sweatpants masking the limbs and their shape. I saw only the thick hands gripping the paddles, pushing them back and dipping them into the inky water, over and over again.

A pile of blankets was in front. My breath caught. Blankets, I said to myself, even as my mind twisted them into the shape of a huddled girl, Screaming Stella or Charlotte or someone else. It was dark; my mind was playing tricks on me. I blinked desperately, trying to shift the image. "Charlotte," I whispered, but I didn't dare raise my voice. She had to be here somewhere. She'd see what I was doing, look at what I was watching, and laugh at me.

"Oh, Bill?" she would say. "He's some recluse that lives down the way. You thought *Bill* had snatched me?" And she would laugh and laugh and laugh, and lead me back to the party.

But seconds passed. And Charlotte did not come.

CHAPTER 7

I couldn't wait forever.

I had to have a plan. As the figure in the rowboat faded towards the horizon, I scrambled down the rocks to the shore, looking for some sign of Charlotte. I thought I could see spaces in the dirt and rock that looked recently trampled on, but I was no detective—it just as easily could have been my imagination playing tricks on me as the clouds rolled past and revealed the pregnant, white moon. My breath came shallow and fast.

I pulled out my phone, hesitated. In my head, the possibilities unspooled: me calling 9-1-1, having a bunch of police officers show up to break up the party, then having Charlotte skip out from the forest, amused and exasperated at what I had done. Or me not calling, and whatever was in that boat disappearing forever (*stop panicking, Reese, don't panic, don't let your imagination run away with you*), taking any sign of Charlotte with it.

I scrolled through my contacts. I didn't have Aiden's number; whatever weirdness was going on between him and his sister that night, I probably would have still called him. Instead I stabbed Riley's name, and the phone began to ring. When we had first exchanged numbers, years ago during our tutoring sessions, I had been so giddy, so embarrassingly hopeful. But Riley's only texts to me were about tutoring, curt and professional.

"Reese?"

I pressed the phone to my ear. "Reese?" Riley's voice came again. I could hear the sounds of the party raging behind him. "Reese? Hello?"

I glanced back at the lake. The rowboat was almost gone, now, a speck in the distance that would soon disappear. I blinked, and could no longer even be sure that the speck *was* the rowboat; the shadows of the night were playing tricks on me.

"I can't find Charlotte," I said. "She ran outside to go to the lake. By herself. And now I can't find her."

"Where are you?"

"By the shore. It's a straight shot—"

"I'll find you," he said. "Stay where you are."

And before I could say anything about the rowboat, he hung up. My heart pounded, and I leaned back towards the cliff, crouching in its shadows. It was so quiet: the water lapped gently at the brown rocks, and occasionally the wind rustled through the dying trees. Not even the sounds of birds or bugs broke through the night. Winter was near, and everything was in decay.

She's fine, I told myself, and indeed, even the act of calling someone else had calmed me down. I had someone else in on my panic, and that lessened it, showed me the places where my fears had run away with me.

But then, the rowboat…

I heard Riley's feet crunching on the stones before I saw him. "Over here," I whispered, and then he emerged from the darkness, dark coat pulled tight around his shoulders, hair a little wild now that the night was mostly gone. His gaze found mine and he stepped quickly forward, and for a moment I thought he meant to hug me. But he zipped past and peered behind my shoulder and then out towards shore.

"I was calling for her," he said, "as I walked over. Didn't spot her. Anything new? Is she answering her phone?"

"Oh," I said, blushing. And then, to cover the fact that I hadn't even thought of that, "Let me try again."

I suppose that I had subconsciously been so sure of the rowboat, so sure of something bad happening, that it hadn't even occurred to me. Stupid. What if I had called her number, and heard it from the boat? I pressed Charlotte's name and put the phone to my ear. Straight to voicemail.

I tried once or twice more, for good measure, putting it on speaker so Riley could hear. Then I shook my head.

"It's alright, we'll find her," Riley said. "She might have passed out somewhere. How much was she drinking?" I realized, with a faint wave of surprise, that he really *was* worried, that he thought the situation serious enough to give up the rest of his enjoyment at the party and help me. But he was trying not to panic.

"I don't know," I said. "But listen—there's something else. Maybe nothing, but…" I swallowed, and told him briefly about the rowboat.

"But you couldn't see who it was?"

"No. Thick hands. That's about it."

"What about frame?" I gave him a blank look, my head too slow to process in the oppressive dark. "Like, big, little? Broad-shouldered?"

"I…don't know. It was dark, kind of hard to tell." I squeezed my eyes shut and tried to remember. "Tall, maybe? I don't know. He was sitting."

"Probably nothing," Riley said, but my stomach somersaulted. He was lying, because he was worried. "Let's check for her in the woods."

"Should we split up?"

"No." His voice was firm, low. "Better if we stay together. Maybe do it in pairs. Can Aiden come help? With someone else."

"Sure. But I don't have his number."

Riley pulled out his phone and dialed. Of course he would have Charlotte's brother's number; they were both athletes, after all, and probably went to all the same parties. And most guys were probably eager to befriend Charlotte Walters' older brother. "Yeah, Aiden, it's Riley," he said. "Listen, Charlotte went into the woods just now, and we can't find her." The voice on the other end rose considerably, and Riley held the phone an inch from his ear. "Yeah, man, Reese and I are going to start combing the woods. We could use your help."

I noticed he said nothing about partners, this time, and after a few more short responses and some vague directions, Riley hung up.

"Well," Riley said lightly. "We'll take care of it."

My mind spun. I focused on trying to remember the

different paths that Charlotte and I used to walk, the different ways that we had gone. "When Aiden comes," I said, "we'll take this side." I swept my arm right, towards the northern half of land. "I know some places she could be…uh, sitting in."

Aiden was full of dark looks and swear words when he joined us. He stared with hostility at Riley, as if it was all his fault. "This better not be some idiotic prank," he snapped.

I rushed to tell him about the rowboat, and only after did I realize how much I had been hoping he would explain it away, tell me that the owner was some neighbor, or that people sailed by in rowboats at midnight all the time. But Aiden looked even more alarmed than Riley. His hand squeezed his phone. "I'll call the police," he said. I looked to Riley, waiting for him to protest, to suggest the search first, but he said nothing. My mouth worked. I felt hot all over. I imagined explaining to the police what I had seen, trying to make them understand why Charlotte had darted out into the night, and why I had been the only one to follow. My heart thumped against my rib cage.

But Aiden did not dial. Finally, obviously just as reluctant as me to face the potential truth of the situation, he said, "We'll search for ten minutes. If we can't find her, I'm calling them."

"That seems reasonable," was all Riley said.

The boys were staring each other down, now. I felt the wave of something deeper there, some thread of history that I wasn't privy to. Then Riley explained that we would take the northern half, which I was more familiar with.

Aiden nodded impatiently and disappeared, winding his way south.

"Ready?" Riley said. His voice was too light, too casual.

We plunged into the forest darkness.

CHAPTER 8

*P*anic is an odd thing. It ebbs and flows like ocean tides, sometimes threatening to swallow you whole, sometimes retreating so far that you felt almost giddy with relief, with the certainty that everything would come out all right.

In our search that night, I thought we had found Charlotte no fewer than three separate times. I caught a glimpse of her behind a tree—or so I thought. I heard her voice call my name—or so I thought. We both heard high-pitched laughter that Riley swore was her—or so he thought.

But no Charlotte.

And every time we didn't find her, every time we skirted around another tree or took another path down to the shore again, tracing back every step Charlotte and I had ever walked on this land, I would think again of the rowboat, and the blanket at the feet of the rower, and I would tell myself *no, no, that's not what it could possibly be.*

"I think," Riley said gently, after forty-five minutes, "I think we'd better call someone."

I glanced at him, eyes widening, no longer able to control my panic. "Maybe Aiden found her," I said, though there was no hope behind my words. I had no hope at all.

"Let's find him," Riley said.

It took us all of twenty minutes. His face fell when he saw us; he had been looking for us, too. Our expressions immediately told each other everything we needed to know.

"Right, then," Aiden said gruffly. "Should have done this an hour ago." He typed in 9-1-1, and I felt dizzy, like I had stepped into an alternate reality. Part of me felt like the pressing of those three buttons were the final summons for Charlotte, the final calling of whatever bluff she could be playing. But Aiden pressed send, and the forest was still.

"Yeah, my sister's missing," Aiden said. "Seventeen. I don't know. An hour. She'd been drinking near the lakeshore. Her friend saw a man out on the water, and we don't know—right. 1301 Windhaven Drive. I'll leave the gate open." He signaled to us to walk towards the house and covered the receiver. "I have to stay on the phone," he said. "Tell people the cops are coming. To clear out. Yeah," he said, back into the receiver. "We were having a party. We're clearing it out now."

He was outwardly calm, but I could see the way his legs shook as he walked, the way his voice had flattened into something that concealed his terror. I wanted to squeeze his shoulder, tell him it would be all right, but that would be all wrong. For a moment I thought, *why couldn't have it*

THE LAST REAL GIRL

been me, instead of Charlotte? Charlotte would have known what to do. She would have found me in an instant, instead of dithering and calling and blindly searching.

Riley did most of the talking, when we were back. He pulled the plug on the speakers and announced that the police were on their way. A ripple of dread and gleeful, drunk excitement followed. Some people ran out without their shoes, or shrieked and grabbed bottles of liquor before dashing into the trees, their laughing and only half-worried friends shouting at them that they were going the wrong way. Many of the kids, duly chastened, gathered their keys and coats methodically and left without a word. Riley rounded up the couples who had ventured upstairs to find bedrooms, and within minutes the whole house had cleared out. I was surprised to find that one of the last people out was Mindy, skirting around the corner of the basement staircase, looking red-faced and keeping her gaze down.

"Right," Riley said. "I should probably go now, too."

He waited, watching me. Of course he would want to leave before the police got here. I understood.

"Thanks," I said. "For helping."

Lights flashed outside. I steeled myself.

"You're not coming?"

I blinked, surprised. It wasn't my house. I hadn't called the police. But the idea of leaving, of not doing anything to find Charlotte, seemed inconceivable to me. "No. I should talk to them."

He hesitated. "Listen," he said, "just be careful about what you say, okay? Don't answer anything if you don't want to."

"Okay," I said, my stomach knotting. Why the sudden concern? We'd be on the same side, the police and I, both trying to find Charlotte.

"I can stay if you want," Riley said.

"No. No, I'll be fine. I'll catch you later."

He hesitated. The doorbell rang, and his head jerked sideways, then back towards me. "You have my number," he said, and I was surprised he remembered—it had been months since our brief, curt texts about study times. Then I remembered—duh. I had just called him. "You'll let me know if you need anything? If I can help at all?" I nodded, and Riley nodded back before spinning on his heel and striding out.

The cop standing at the door, young and wiry and black, watched Riley as he disappeared. For a moment, it seemed to me that they had nodded slightly at one another, not just the polite nod of two strangers acknowledging each other's presence, but the subtle one of recognition. The cop frowned; Riley hurried off.

I felt rather than saw Aiden appear at my shoulder. I didn't look at him; instead, I watched the cop closely. He seemed deep in thought for a moment, so much so that it took him half a beat to take Aiden's outstretched hand.

"Officer Bordeaux. I understand your sister's missing?"

CHAPTER 9

I had thought that cops weren't meant to take you seriously, when you told them that a young girl was missing—especially at a house party with drinking involved. I had expected someone who would come in and ask rude questions about Charlotte's alcohol consumption and overall unreliability, and then tell us to call again in a few days if she didn't show up.

Officer Bordeaux was not like that at all. Nor was his partner, Officer Stone, a dark-haired young woman with a long nose and deep brown eyes, who had Aiden sit down on a couch in front of half-full beer cans and some questionable-looking cigarettes, focusing on him with calm intensity and the serious demeanor of someone who was not just responding out of some eye-roll-inducing sense of duty.

I fluttered nearby, not sure if I was wanted or needed, but Officer Stone called me over almost immediately. That surprised me too; from my television-show understanding of these things, wouldn't they need to question us separately? But the officers dug in right away: where had we seen Charlotte last? Had she been drinking? What did the figure in the rowboat look like? Did anyone else see him?

I felt, above all, that we had entered some alternate world. The cops had an air of unreality about them, like they were hired actors that were taking their roles too seriously. The clock struck midnight in the middle of our conversation, great fat chimes on the grandfather clock in the living room, and we all jumped at the sudden sound. As if in answer, the wind howled against the floor-to-ceiling windows looking into the Walters' backyard, and a few of the bottles on the glass end table shook and shivered.

"Well," Officer Bordeaux said, when the wind died down. "It sounds like we'd better have a look."

Aiden rose, and I followed.

"You guys sit tight," Officer Stone said. "We need you here in case Charlotte comes back. I'll write my cell down so you can give me a call if she does."

Aiden took the proffered number with a grimace. "We already checked a lot of the forest," he said. "The spots she usually would go to. I could get out our boat, take a look on the water…"

"You have a boat?" Officer Stone said, with mild interest. But I caught the steel look in her eye.

"Yeah, a rowboat. But Charlotte wouldn't have taken it," he added, defensively, when now Officer Bordeaux wheeled to face him. "She hates that thing. Says it's always slopping water over the sides. We only ever used it when we were kids, anyway, before my dad got the motorboat."

"Is the motorboat nearby?"

"No. My dad sold it a few months ago."

"Ah. Why's that?"

A cloud came over Aiden's face. I was sure that the cop noticed it too. "He just didn't need it anymore," Aiden muttered. "Waste of time."

"But not the rowboat?"

"Who's going to buy some old rowboat? Wouldn't be worth the time to sell it."

Officer Stone and Officer Bordeaux exchanged a glance. *What?* I wanted to shout at them. *What are you thinking? What does that mean?* Did they think that Charlotte had gone for a midnight row? That someone had taken the boat from Charlotte's house? I was with the cops on one point: Aiden should have brought this up sooner, the very moment I mentioned seeing a rowboat on the water.

But the cops left through the back door, and Aiden sank back onto the couch.

"Do you think it was your boat I saw?" I asked, after some hesitation.

Aiden dropped his head into his hands. "Maybe? I don't know. I didn't think—it's been years since I saw that thing. I forgot we even had one, until a few minutes ago." He swore. "Charlotte isn't pulling something on us? Some prank?"

The hope in his voice made me queasy. "No," I said. "I mean, not that she told me about."

Aiden pulled out his phone, hesitated. "I should call my parents," he said. "But there's nothing they can do right now, and besides—" He frowned, and then for one awful moment looked like he might cry. The moment passed, and I wondered if I had imagined it. "It'll wait. Their flight home is tomorrow morning. Not like they can rush that."

"Where are they?" I said, just to make conversation. I began picking up beer cans and bottles, too, for something to do with my hands.

"Does it matter?"

"No. I was just asking."

Aiden shrugged. He dropped his head into his hands again and swore once more. "What is *wrong* with this family," he said, and I carried the bottles to the sink, afraid now that he really might be crying.

I snuck a glance at him as I rinsed out the bottles. My relationship with Charlotte's brother had always been basically nonexistent. He was a year older than us, for one, which meant that we never saw him in classes and kept to the individual divide of the student center where seniors ate lunch in one corner, juniors another, and so on. He was tall and good-looking and athletic and smart—every blessing you could ask for—and that also put him, for me, less into the category of human being and more into the category of some otherworldly creature that I needn't bother trying to even talk to. And though he and Charlotte seemed to get along most of the time, they never hung out together or had the same friends, and he was never more than coolly polite to me, never nice enough or interested enough to make my indifference flutter and fan out into something stronger, more dangerous.

And then he had spent so much time home, his freshman fall, that I had known to avoid the topic with Charlotte entirely. There was a wrongness about it that I did not dare address, and that Charlotte showed no eagerness to fill me in on. Family stuff, I thought. Everyone had it.

I returned for more bottles and snuck another glance at Aiden. He wasn't crying after all, but his face had a pale, hollow, haunted look. I thought about earlier that night, when he had been so protective about Charlotte wandering out to see Screaming Stella.

"Were you…worried, earlier?" I ventured. "When you wanted to go with us to the water?"

"Of course," Aiden said, with an annoyed shrug. "It's stupid to go anywhere near water when you're drunk."

"But you didn't think…"

"I didn't know she was going to disappear, no." His gaze snapped up to me, full of rage. He sucked in a long breath. "Sorry. I just—"

"It's fine. I understand." I paused, holding a beer bottle in my right hand and two others tucked beneath my arm. "It's going to be okay," I said, because it seemed someone should be saying things like that, sounding optimistic, not rushing to think the worst. That had never been me before, but I could play that role now. After all, wasn't it just as likely that was the case? "She'll turn up soon. And probably be annoyed we called the police on her."

Aiden snorted, but the sadness rushed back into his face almost just as fast. "If you want, you can stay in the guest room," he said. He didn't look up at me, only leaning over his knees and staring at the ground. "I know it's kind of late to go home. I don't know if you can drive."

"I didn't drink much. But yeah, I'll stay, maybe help you look in the morning?"

We both winced. That meant acknowledging the fact

that perhaps the police would return empty-handed, that this ordeal was not over.

"Sure," Aiden said. And then, finally looking up at me, "Thanks."

I looked away first; his blue gaze was too much like Charlotte's, and they had the same sloping nose, the fine-boned features, the gentle waves of dark hair. I felt a strong and sudden urge to see her, to know she was okay, and a wave of panic threatened to overtake me. I covered it by busying myself again with the bottles, waving off Aiden's protest that he'd do it in the morning. A few minutes later, my phone chimed.

Riley.

Everything okay? Any sign?

I hesitated, wondering if I should leave it until the morning, when we had a real update. But I texted quickly back: *All fine. Still looking for her. Cops are nice.* I reread it, deleted the last line, and pressed send.

His reply was almost instantaneous.

Okay. Text if you need anything.

If I needed anything? It felt a little odd, under the circumstances. And, I thought, a little too worried. For all we knew, Charlotte was just passed out under a tree some-where. So why was Riley acting so sure it was something else?

Why did I feel so sure it was, too?

CHAPTER 10

*I*t was after two when the police left; they promised more help tomorrow and told us to call them directly if we heard anything. They also asked us to call Charlotte's phone, but each time it went straight to voicemail.

"Let us know if you find it," Officer Stone said. I thought she seemed more solemn than Officer Bordeaux, a little more urgent. Officer Bordeaux, on the other hand, seemed cool and calm and confident, as if this was a problem that could be solved with quick efficiency. I found myself imagining their working relationship, picturing them out on a call together, Officer Bordeaux strolling smoothly into a dangerous situation while Officer Stone assessed and calculated with fierce intelligence from the squad car before striking like a snake.

Aiden directed me to one of the spare bedrooms on the second floor, one that looked like some staged room in a designer sample home. "Looks like no one's been messing about in here," he said, then blushed and muttered some-

59

thing about going to find me a towel for the shower. "Through here," he said, returning, pointing to the en suite bathroom just around the corner. "There's new toothbrushes and toothpaste and stuff, too."

"Thanks," I said. He had probably forgotten that I had stayed there before, many times, though in Charlotte's room rather than the spare. Compared to the rigid lines and sharp corners of the spare room, Charlotte's was all soft edges and pillowy comforters and deep sea-green fabrics. Though a housekeeper came in every two weeks to attempt to apply order, Charlotte's things kept spilling out of every edge: clothes piled on top of her swivel chair, makeup clustering on top of her oak wardrobe, jewelry cast carelessly beneath a beaded lamp. I thought of it, empty now, and had to fight the rising wave of panic again. She'd be here, soon. We'd find her.

It was hard to fall asleep that night. Every scratch, every howl of the wind outside, seemed to me to be Charlotte crying out. I would begin to doze, only to awaken with a shudder and a bolt of terror, certain that I had heard her step in the hallway, that I had felt her shadow darken my door. I considered flicking on the lamp next to my bed and sleeping in half-light, like I used to do as a kid when I thought it was the only thing that would beat back the ghosts from my bed. But I was too paralyzed with my panic to do anything, and so I lay there, counting the minutes until morning, occasionally falling into patches of fitful sleep.

At some point, I must have settled in and fallen into a deeper slumber, for I woke with a start at a creak just outside my door—real this time, loud and distinct, different than the phantom ones I had been hearing half the night.

I froze. My breath caught in my lungs as I strained my ears for any other noises. What if, I thought, whatever had come for Charlotte was now coming for me?

A shadow stretched and shimmered into my room. I felt wildly for my phone, fingers trembling, wondering how long it would take my shaking hands to open the lock screen, then the calling app, then dial 9-1-1. Or I could click emergency call—but would that be quick enough? Would I accidentally open the phone when my thumb touched the home button? My mouth was swollen and dry. My fingers still had not found the phone, but I didn't dare take my eyes off of my bedroom door.

The knob began to turn. Abandoning my stillness, and any hope I had that I was imagining what I was seeing, I cast myself towards the nightstand, scrambling for my phone. The door creaked open just as I managed to snatch the phone, and I had just unlocked it to dial the police when a voice said:

"Trouble sleeping, too?"

My knees buckled beneath me. My shoulders sagged. "Aiden," I half-gasped. Again his likeness to his sister made something eerie and strange in the deep night; if I looked up at his face in the dark shadows, I could see Charlotte's bright eyes staring back at me, Charlotte's lips laughing at me and my obvious fear.

But Aiden was not laughing; he looked somber and exhausted, and made his way over to the side of my bed. I replaced the phone on the nightstand.

"I keep thinking I hear her, or see her," he murmured.

"Do you mind?"

"What? Oh, no, not at all."

Aiden grunted and lowered himself into the armchair next to my bed. There was a knitted blanket thrown over the back that he unfolded and stretched across his lap, even as he rested his head back against the dark cushions.

I left him in silence, still too shocked that the quiet and moody Aiden Walters had walked into my bedroom and sat down next to me. It only heightened my sense that we had entered some strange world where everything was upside-down, where reality was taken, churned up, and cast back out like the reflection of a distorted funhouse mirror. After a few minutes, my eyes began to flutter shut again; it *was* easier to sleep with him in the room, as it had been easier to fall asleep at sleepovers or with my mother when I was a kid and still afraid of monsters beneath the bed. Another consciousness nearby dispelled my imagination, made my brain more rationally weigh each creak and flutter, dismissing most.

"I really don't want to tell my parents," Aiden said, and my eyes blinked open again. Sleep slipped further away from me once more.

"About Charlotte?"

"Yes." A pause, where Aiden shifted on the armchair, and I held my breath. The hour was late—the witching hour, as Charlotte used to say. We had entered a space when things went topsy-turvy, when unwritten rules could be broken, when secrets could come out. "They're dealing with enough right now. This is the last thing they need. They—" He swore again and let his face drop into his hands.

I pulled myself up, thankful that I didn't have a change of clothes and so was still in my bra and t-shirt from the night before, even though the former had been digging into my back for half the night. Better than pajamas, though, with their flimsy fabrics and thin comforts. At least I could reach over for Aiden's arm, as I did now, without worrying about spilling out of this or revealing too much of that.

I felt awkward and clumsy, but forced myself to grab his forearm and squeeze in what I hoped was a comforting gesture. When I pulled my hand back he grabbed it, fingers closing over mine, tight and shaking.

My heart thrummed in my chest. I adjusted myself up in bed so that I could better hold his hand, feeling that strange sense of unreality as I did so. I felt guilty for the way my heart sped up at his touch, for how I noticed the warmth and smoothness and strength of his grip. He needed comfort, that was all, and since I had never held hands with a boy, not properly, my hormones were going mad, and I'd just have to clamp down on them. Simple.

"We'll keep looking," I said to him. "We'll find her."

"I should have been protecting her," he said. "I wasn't paying attention. I got distracted—"

"Aiden, you couldn't have known. None of us did. I mean, I was out the door thirty seconds after her, and I couldn't find her." I felt a stab of guilt at this and winced as I looked up at his face, trying to read any expression of blame there. For if anyone could have caught up with Charlotte, saved us from this whole ordeal, it was me. And I had failed.

But Aiden just shook his head, gaze still downcast.

"She didn't—she didn't talk about doing anything stupid, recently?"

He looked up at me. His eyes were shiny, glazed with tears, and in the darkness he looked like some woodland fairy-tale creature that had floated in to perch next to my bed and whisper secrets. "Anything stupid," I repeated, half-stuttering. "No—no! Of course not. But why do you think—"

"Charlotte can be unpredictable," Aiden said. His gaze was searching mine. I forced myself to hold it, to show that I was not hiding anything, that he could trust me. But it was like staring at the sun; I wanted to blink and look away, afraid that everything inside me would burn up if I did not. "There are things...I didn't know how she was handling it all, not really. She seemed to take it well, but she wouldn't tell me if she didn't, would she?"

I didn't respond. Were Charlotte's parents, I thought, getting a divorce? It seemed like the kind of problem a girl like her would have—parents, with their giant bank accounts and great portfolio of properties, dividing assets and zipping off to lawyers' meetings, making cool accusations about mistresses and veiled threats about child support or alimony.

Finally, I said, "She seemed perfectly happy. She was all excited about the party tonight."

Aiden shrugged. It was obvious that he didn't quite believe me, and I began to doubt myself. Had Charlotte been perfectly happy? Had there been a twinge of reckless-ness in her insistence on having the party, at such short notice, and at having things like the keg there, which we had never done before? But why not? We were seniors—we were supposed to be a bit stupid this year.

My hand was still in Aiden's, who had not loosened his grip. I wondered if it was up to me to gently extricate myself, if at some point his churning mind would pause long enough to realize what he had done, and cast my hand away like some encroaching bug.

Just to break the silence, I added, "There was one thing, though, I didn't know about. She didn't want Mindy at the party. Though," I said quickly, lest my piece of information sound too melodramatic, too conspiracy theory-esque, "she saw her later in the night and didn't kick her out or anything. She just kind of avoided her."

Aiden glanced up at me again, eyes searching mine. The information didn't seem to come as a surprise to him —interesting. "They were fighting, you think?" he said carefully.

"Well, I suppose so. I don't think she's ever had a problem with Mindy before. Maybe it's some field hockey stuff?" Though I couldn't imagine why Charlotte would fight about field hockey. She had not cared about it one whit this year, skipping preseason week, shrugging off game-day duties to wear uniforms and special outfits and sell candy bars for the fundraiser, telling me that it didn't matter anymore; she wasn't going to play in college, so why waste all of her time? But, she attended every practice and game, and I knew that she was still one of the team's top scorers, enough to earn her spot as captain for that year.

But a fight with Mindy? No, it wouldn't fit into that.

"Maybe," Aiden said. But it was obvious he had dismissed the possibility of her involvement; whatever had happened to Charlotte, he believed Mindy had nothing to do with it. I felt silly for even bringing the topic up.

"You knew Charlotte better than almost anyone," Aiden said, after another minute of silence. My skin prickled. Did I? I was her best friend, sure, but Aiden was family, flesh and blood. He knew the way she carried her secrets, could read the fleeting emotions in each change of expression, because he did the same thing, too. I'd always be an outsider, when it came to the Walters. "Where do— what do you think happened?"

He looked desperate, almost hopeful as he watched me, waiting for an answer. I swallowed. "I…I'm not sure. I think maybe she went to play some trick, or something. Maybe twisted her ankle." Or worse. "It'll be easier to look for her in the morning. I can help."

"Some trick?"

"Yeah, just a prank maybe, or something. She wanted me to follow her. Charlotte's always got one prank or another going on." Like releasing crickets into the media center, or roping off the entire junior parking lot one morning with the words "UNDER CONSTRUCTION" printed on a paper taped to the cones.

"Maybe," Aiden said doubtfully. He shifted in the armchair and released my hand to catch the blanket as it slid off of his lap. I let it hover nearby for a second, not sure what the protocol now was, before pulling it back towards me and thrusting it under the covers. "Thanks for staying, Reese. It's—thanks. If anyone could find her… She always says the nicest things about you, you know. About how smart you are. How nice. After those girls—" He shook his head. "You probably know."

I blushed. "It's no problem, really."

"I'm glad she's friends with someone like you." Someone like me? Someone not popular or glamorous enough, he meant, to compete with Charlotte, to tear her down? "She deserves a good friend. Someone loyal."

"Charlotte's been a great friend to me," I said cautiously. "I'm lucky to have her."

Again his gaze bored into mine. "You're a nice person," he said, and it almost didn't sound like praise, coming from his lips. "That's not as common as you think. It's probably why she's so protective of you."

"Protective?"

A ghost of a smile flitted over his face, gone just as soon as it appeared. "Yeah, I'll let her explain, when she's back." The reminder sobered us both, and a heavy silence descended.

"Do you mind if I sleep here for a bit?" Aiden said. His voice was soft, a little shaky. "I can't sleep well in my room. I keep thinking that I see her."

"No, of course not. Do you need a pillow, or something?"

I handed him one of the six that was littered around my bed, and he reclined the chair, drawing his blanket up to his neck. I watched him for a second, wondering what exactly he was worried about Charlotte worrying about, wondering where Charlotte had gone, wondering if the morning light would bring an end to it all.

My right hand, the one that Aiden's had held, tingled beneath my blanket. I thrust down the thoughts that rose up in my mind and closed my eyes to sleep.

CHAPTER 11

I called my mom early in the morning, updating her as much as I dared. She, understandably, did not take the news of a missing girl very well, and had to be talked out of skipping her next shift to come over and help me look. It was exactly what I didn't want: my mother, grim-faced and sighing and troubled, stalking around the Walters' house and asking us questions that the police had already put to us, making us retrace steps we had already walked.

It wasn't that my mother was bad in a crisis—she was a nurse, after all, and she kept a level head. She was methodical, stalwart. But I feared seeing her face, seeing reflected in her expression all of the fear and worry that I was trying so desperately to master. And I feared Aiden seeing that, too.

In the end, I convinced her that there was nothing that she could do to help anyway, and besides, she had already missed a shift last week when her brother, my Uncle

Garrett, had gone to the hospital after a roofing accident (broken foot, all around not quite so bad as we had feared when the paramedics had been making noises about his back).

"Who's that?" a voice said behind me, just as I hung up. I jumped.

"My mom," I said, turning around to face Aiden. I was seated on one of the kitchen stools, ivory base and smooth leather cushion, the kind with the little flare at the bottom that was some smug nod to back support. "Just updating her." I resisted the urge to smooth back my wild hair or tug at my wrinkled clothes, the same ones I had worn yesterday and to bed. At least I had found an unopened deodorant in the guest bathroom to use, placed neatly next to a set of other designated toiletries for visitors.

Aiden looked pale and haggard in the morning light, dressed in a navy bathrobe. He kept his distance from me, I noted, and there was nothing of the openness of the night before. Quickly gathering it would be best to pretend it had never happened at all, I said, "Should we split up the forest again? Keep looking, now that it's light?"

"Yes. That sounds good." His voice was dull. "I-I should call my parents first."

"I'll step outside," I said quickly. "Give you some privacy."

I threw on my jacket and walked out onto the patio, sliding the glass door closed behind me. The morning air was chilly, the fall sun illuminating a white and cloudless sky. I stomped around for a bit, trying to warm myself, before half-turning back to the window. Aiden was pacing around the kitchen in his robe, a deep frown on his face.

He was listening, mostly, occasionally adding a word or two. I pictured the Walters on the other end of the phone call, worried, nearly hysterical. Probably demanding to know why he hadn't called them immediately, though I privately agreed that he had done what was best, that there was no way for them to get an earlier flight, and he at least had saved them from being sleep-deprived when they arrived home.

Finally, Aiden hung up the phone. He caught my eye and waved me inside. "I'm going to change," he said stonily. "Then we can search."

We ended up splitting the area north and south again, and parting just outside the house. I thrust my hands into my pockets and hurried along the perimeter of the property, determined to search my portion properly, in the day's light. The mystical enchantment of the forest—and all of its hauntings—had been beaten back by the sun, and suddenly everything seemed possible to me, if only I was careful enough. I trudged back and forth along the lines of trees, not once getting lost, not once missing my turns. And then I reached the shore, where I paused at the top of the rocks and looked down, trying to imagine a rowboat bobbing on the smooth, iron-colored water.

Where are you, Charlotte, I thought. *Just give me a sign.*

I waited, but to no avail. The magic of the place wasn't active during the day, for better or for worse. And so I turned and walked back to the house, where I found Aiden waiting for me inside. He pushed a cup of coffee towards me.

"Anything?" he said, trying to sound casual and failing.

"Nothing. You?"

"No. Though I thought…well."

"Thought what?"

"Yesterday. When we were searching. I swore I saw someone running through the trees. I *heard* something, for sure, some rustling or whatnot. But I don't know."

"When? Before the cops came?"

"No, after. I just stepped onto the patio—I don't know. I was listening hard for her. Maybe it was my imagination."

"Still," I said, drawing the coffee towards me. I could smell almond and something sharper, like cinnamon, and took a deep breath. "You should tell the police. Anything could be helpful."

"I suppose."

I could tell by the way he said it that he wouldn't tell them. That faraway look was back now; I guessed that he was thinking about his parents.

"What time are they coming?" I said.

He looked up at me, blue eyes even brighter next to the navy sweater he had on, a white collar popped out of it. On some guys the outfit would look middle-aged and professorial, but it hung off Aiden's thin, wiry frame like a stylish snapshot from a magazine. Charlotte was the same way: everything she wore looked like cutting-edge fashion.

"This afternoon," he said. His gaze on mine felt intense, questioning. I couldn't hold it for long.

"Well," I said. And hesitated. What was the right thing to do here? I wanted desperately to keep looking for Charlotte, to search for clues, but I didn't want to overstay my welcome. And I couldn't imagine being back here when the Walters arrived, raw in their grief. "What do you think? Where else should we look?"

Something like relief flitted across Aiden's face. "I thought the boathouse, where we keep the rowboat," Aiden said. "The police will want to know if it's missing anyway. If—" He let the words remain unspoken: *if someone did steal it, and possibly Charlotte with it.* "And then along the shore... Maybe she dropped something, or someone... Anyway."

"Okay," I said. "That's a good idea. And then maybe the treehouse?" I called it a treehouse, but we both knew it was nothing like it at all: just a twisted old tree, with branches that looped and curved and dipped every which way, made for easy climbing. It was one property over, a bit of the way down, but we had often stopped there in middle school: if you climbed high enough, you could see to the vegetation-covered islands in the middle of the lake.

"Right," Aiden said, straightening. "The treehouse! I forgot all about that." He poured our coffee in to-go mugs, offering me cream, which I accepted, and sugar, which I declined. I noticed he took his coffee the same way, and I felt a moment of something like pride and an even more ridiculous emotion that I didn't even want to investigate. Just because you like coffee the same way, I chastised myself, doesn't mean you're destined to become friends.

"What is it?" Aiden said, slipping his coat back on. "Everything okay?"

I had to be cheery, optimistic. Not let him know the depth of the dread that was now my constant companion. "Yes, of course. Let's go."

In the end, we spent two hours in near silence walking

the shore, heading out to the treehouse and finding nothing but empty beach. Our last stop was to the boathouse—I think we both were dreading it—and I almost couldn't look as Aiden pulled the (unlocked) doors open.

The rowboat was gone.

CHAPTER 12

You free to meet up? Need to talk. Important.

I blinked down at my phone, trying to make sense of Riley's text. It was nearly four; Aiden's parents had no doubt arrived home, had had their first good cry in the house now empty of their daughter. I had not been able to focus since I came back, worrying about whether there was anywhere else I could have searched, anything else I could have done. I had called Charlotte's phone another half-dozen times, and each call clicked straight to voicemail.

About Charlotte? I said. If it wasn't, I would put Riley off. I had only slept fitfully and intermittently the night before, and it was catching up with me. I could feel the heaviness dragging on the corners of my eyes.

Sort of.

I rolled my eyes and tossed my phone across the bed. Sort of. It pinged a few seconds later, and I groaned, stretching my fingers for it.

Just something to be careful of.

I reread the message a few times. My curiosity was piqued, certainly, but something seemed off about the messages. They were vague, a little cryptic. I had an instinct that if I met up with Riley, he wouldn't tell me what he meant: he would give me carefully veiled warnings about things that I should or should not do, and I didn't have time to waste.

Part of me marveled at the sudden change in my thinking: if Riley Gallagher had been texting me two days before, I would have been freaking out, screenshotting each piece of the conversation to send to Charlotte for dissection. But now Charlotte wasn't here, and what's more, I had bigger things on my plate than trying to decipher a boy's strange texts. I wanted directness, and I wanted answers—in all things.

You can call me, I said. *Or text. Can't get out today.*

The response was almost immediate. *Tomorrow morning? Before school?*

I hesitated. But I was curious. *Sure.*

I reread the chain again. *Something to be careful of,* Riley had said. A prickle went up my spine. I wondered, for the first time, what people at the party had seen. What other people might know.

I squeezed the phone in my hand. Tomorrow, when I went back to school, I'd find out.

CHAPTER 13

It was all wrong, climbing into my mother's car early in the morning, tucking my legs over the change of clothes that she had brought—beige cardigan and plain jeans, so she could do her shopping after without looking like she was advertising her services in a medical emergency. My shoulders hunched, my knees drew up to my chest, and I laid my head back against the prickly cloth headrest, inhaling the scents of stale pine and dog hair and faint grease from when one of us had last gone through the Freddie Fry drive-thru.

Charlotte had been driving me for as long as I could remember; the only times my mom had dropped me off had been when Charlotte was sick (rare) or when Charlotte's car was in the shop (rarer). I felt like a little kid again, like the nervous middle schooler slouching in the front seat every morning before my mother rolled up to school—a block away, so she could avoid most of the traffic—and told me that she loved me, and could I catch the bus home?

The sedan rumbled to a noisy stop. My mother shifted the car into park and looked over at me. She seemed serene, almost otherworldly, in the bright morning light, her blonde wispy hair tucked into a neat low bun, her pale hands scrubbed clean, skin chafed near the fingernails, her scrubs a cross between official robes and elevated pajamas—one of the greatest perks, she always said, of her job. Her hazel eyes blinked at me like a bird's, intelligent and inquisitive. I knew she wanted to ask me about Charlotte, to press me more than she had the night before. I'm sure to her it was like any other problem that we had to solve, that required just enough thought and grim decision-making to resolve it: how would we pay the bills once Dad and his scattered child support checks disappeared (*she'd renew her license and go back to work, of course*), how would I manage if she took a job across the state for a much better pay in a much better area (*we'd uproot, naturally, and follow the money*), how would we find housing in an area that seemed so wholly and creepily wary of outsiders, like some ancient cult or inbred family that was loathe to accept us (*she'd contact some churches and women's groups, not be too proud to accept the charity that was offered*).

But Charlotte—Charlotte was not a problem that could just be solved through a series of methodical steps and resigned actions. I tensed, waiting for my mother to speak. I almost wanted her to say something that I could twist into the ugly, some words that cut deep in the morning air, that would tilt me out of this nightmare and fill me with rage, black and raw, that I could throw back at her, at someone.

But my mother sighed, and said, "I love you, Reese. You take care of yourself, okay?"

I deflated. It meant, some part of me whispered, that she thought there was nothing at all to do about Charlotte. That she had already given her up as irrevocably lost. "Love you," I said, and slipped out the door, into the biting air and frost that my mother was still trying to beat back from the windowshield, little fractured ice crystals climbing up the front of the glass. I thrust my hands into my pockets as the car rumbled away.

The sky was a blinding gray-white as I trudged the block towards school, joining swarms of kids in backpacks and on skateboards and bikes and other annoying wheeled contraptions as we funneled ourselves towards the sprawling brick campus covered in swathes of ivy. I remembered when I had first arrived at St. Clair and had thought the whole town seemed like a storybook. All the public buildings, town hall and schools and whatnot, were white stone or red brick, surrounded by wrought iron gates or else heavy stone walls, with pebbled paths and mani-cured lawns and bronze plaques in front of little statues of people or horses or dogs that had some special importance to St. Clair that the plaques never adequately explained (*Mighty, dog, 1941-1954. Loyal protector of the White Willow. Cherished pet of Richard and Misty Simmons*). Even the little shops downtown were all quaint and unique: no chains, the city had ordained, and no fast food restaurants—you had to go one town over for Freddie Fry. Instead of greasy burgers you could get hand-crafted Mediterranean wraps, instead of industrial soft serve you could get slow-churned local ice cream in one of twelve different seasonal flavors (pumpkin pie icing, spiked apple cider, and dark chocolate pecan pie, among others, for this fall), instead of your local chain coffee, you could get slow-drip hipster nonsense, where you paid twice as much for something that took five times as long delivered in cups stamped with the company's logo of a wolf's paw with an eye in the bottom pad.

All that to say, St. Clair was not your typical place. I knew that, and I loved the town for it, even though I had been determined at first to sulk for months and hate the place for years. It was beautiful, and strange, and charming, full of secrets and side streets and little hidden surprises that you had to learn only over time, when someone deeper into the town lore than you could point out the hidden lakeshore path, or take you down to the yacht club at the back of the city park that you did not even know was there.

Charlotte had been my guide, the person who had unlocked all of the secrets of St. Clair for me. She was not stingy or suspicious, not hesitant or possessive. She seemed to take some pleasure in my plain, unself-conscious delight in St. Clair; I used to think that she, like everyone else in this town, had grown to take it for granted, and perhaps she liked the reminder again of how lucky she was, how blessed.

Now that it was just me, though, walking up to the steps of the school, passing the lion statues with their teeth bared guarding either side of the stairs, I couldn't help remembering how I had felt in those first few weeks after we moved, before Charlotte decided to befriend me and welcome me into the town. Everything had a sinister cast: the secrets were not charming, but threatening. The faces of the people swarming before me were closed, unreadable. The whole of the place—iron railings, stone steps, great big heavy wooden doors that closed with a quick *whoosh*—seemed oddly alive, furtive, full of secrets, as if a thousand unseen eyes were watching me and wondering what I thought I was doing there.

I shuddered as I pushed inside, into the warm dry heat of the school. A chandelier hung high above the entryway, butter yellow light casting diamond patterns on the floor and walls, cobwebs of shadows in between. I ducked and weaved my way into the student center, a great cavern like something out of a college or prep school film, with horizontal wooden tables and stone floors and stained-glass windows, the walls peppered with posters and announcements and bright green school jerseys that contrasted sharply with the medieval feel.

"Hey," Riley said, peeling off one of the back walls and falling into step with me. "Want to grab a table?"

I followed him to the middle of one of the long wooden tables, where we both tucked our legs over the low benches and leaned across the scarred wood so that we were close enough not to be overheard. I thought I could feel people watching me and tried not to get jumpy, though my fingers twitched. And I swore the whisper of *Charlotte* snaked across the room.

"You had something to tell me?" I said.

Riley blinked, nodded. It was odd sitting so close to him again, like back when I had tutored him. He had always been attentive, polite, leaning forward in the study hall room so that his sleeve nearly touched mine. But he had been always distracted, too, ready to crack jokes to make the teacher or one of his buddies laugh, wide-ranging in his attention, as if he couldn't settle down and focus on the math, or on me.

Now, it was different. Riley looked like he had forgotten the rest of the world existed. His face was close to mine, close enough that I could see the blond whiskers that he had not bothered to shave that morning, could smell the citrus shampoo that he must have used on his still-wet hair. His brown eyes were locked on mine, intent, serious.

"Something about Charlotte?" I prompted. I didn't do well with silence; I was too fidgety, too nervous.

Riley's gaze broke away. It took a few seconds for him to draw himself up, look back at me. "Yeah, well," he said, "did you guys find anything?"

"No."

Riley's jaw tightened. "Who was looking?"

I thought you were hear to tell me *info*, I thought. But I said, "Me and Aiden. And the police."

"Good. They were there the whole time?"

"At night. Then Aiden and I looked some more in the morning. You were going to—"

"You and Aiden, by yourselves?" Riley said sharply.

No, with a pink unicorn, I wanted to snap, but I took a breath and steadied myself. The number of eyes on us only seemed to be growing, and I felt beads of sweat forming at the back of my neck. "Yes, just the two of us. I left before his parents got back." My mother had had to take a ride share to work that day, something that I had received surprisingly little flak about, all things considered. I had picked her up that night.

"By ourselves," I confirmed. "Riley, what are you—"

"Sorry," he said, with a quick shake of his head. "I don't mean to—I mean, I don't know anything about what happened to Charlotte. I just want you to be careful." His eyes searched mine, looking for something in them, I thought, that certainly wasn't there. I had no idea what he was talking about, what he was trying to tell me, and I found myself growing angry and impatient. My friend was gone; I didn't need more secrets and cryptic hints that amounted to nothing more than the same advice my mother had given me when I'd left that morning.

"Right," I said, starting to untuck my legs from the bench. "Will do. Thanks."

"Hold on," Riley said, reaching out to catch my arm. His fingers rested lightly and briefly on my forearm, and my skin prickled. My mind flashed immediately to Aiden, in the middle of the night, hand snatching out to hold mine, face vulnerable and alone in the dark and cavernous house.

Riley blushed and withdrew his hand, but I remained poised on the cusp of leaving, waiting. Before all this, before Charlotte had disappeared, I probably would never have dared to leave Riley seated alone. I would have stayed for every scrap of attention and time he was willing to give me, enthralled that he seemed to be taking some sort of interest in me, in what I was doing. But none of that mattered now; what mattered was Charlotte, and getting her back.

"I shouldn't be telling you any of this," Riley said, his voice so low that I had to bend my head forward, hair falling over my chin, to hear him. He leaned forward, too, so that his words snaked right into my ear. "Danny and

Aiden. Just be careful of them, okay? Try not to be with them alone, if you can help it."

"What?"

"I said, try not to—"

"No, I heard you. Why?"

I leaned back enough to catch a glimpse of Riley's face, a thousand emotions scuttling over its surface. "I can't explain, not now," he said. "I just—they might have been involved in something, last year."

"What does that have to do with Charlotte?"

He looked pained. "I can't explain it, not right now. If I could—just, don't be with them alone, okay? Call me and I'll come with you, if you're doing any more searches, or anything."

I scanned his face. He seemed deadly serious, a little embarrassed, perhaps, but earnest.

"Why?" I pressed again. But Riley shook his head, and then the bell rang, and the whole world began to swarm with movement.

CHAPTER 14

*R*iley's warning echoed in my head as I drifted off to class, one ghost among many, footsteps echoing across the cavernous hall as faces haunted by insomnia or exams or social woes or more ducked into the various wings of the school. The whole thing was madness —Riley's warning, Charlotte's disappearance, like a bad prank gone wrong.

The strange thing was, that morning, I had woken up with a new feeling blooming within me. I would have thought, before it all happened, that the disappearance of Charlotte would diminish me, cow me, that I would suddenly become invisible because my one claim to identity—*Charlotte's best friend*—had been stripped from me, and I had been laid bare to the high school pecking order that would chew me up and spit me out. I had thought that the severing of that tenuous connection (however temporary, it had to be temporary) would leave me scuttling from room to room, head down, shoulders hunched, aware now that

my greatest ally, my greatest protection, my greatest confi-
dante, was nowhere to be found.

That's what I had expected, and it came as a surprise
to me to find that I had gotten it all wrong.

Strangely, I think it was because, in the crisis, I was
thinking less of myself in general. And that didn't diminish
me—it made me more whole. Stronger.

I felt eyes slide to me during class, felt the pointed
fingers and the whispers that darted behind my back. But I
did not back down. I met the gazes, I turned around to see
the person who was whispering. Normally it would be
Charlotte who whipped around, lazy half-grin dripping off
her face, to ask someone what was so funny in a voice that
made it clear you'd better let her in on the joke. But now
there was no one, and Charlotte needed protecting. I was
the one who looked back at the whispering heads and
cocked one eyebrow. *What is it?* I mouthed, a couple times,
head cocked and forehead knit, leaning towards them like I
was ready to be taken into their confidence. The heads
would drop, the faces would sober, the whispers would
silence for the rest of class.

At lunch, I walked straight to the library, which
normally would have given me hot flashes, paranoid that a
thousand pairs of eyes were on me, watching me shame
walk my way out of lunch and its social pressures, such as
on days when Charlotte was sick and I didn't feel like
making nice with any of the girls I'd played freshman
soccer with, before succumbing to the fact that I wasn't any
good. But now I spared the walk not a second thought; I
took my sandwich and dipped into the farthest computer
room, where you could sneak drinks and snacks if you

were careful, and powered up the back left computer, blue light glowing in the dim room, crumbs scattered on the patterned white carpet beneath my feet.

I searched her name, first. Nothing. "Missing girl St. Clair" led to some old articles, a year back, nothing about Charlotte and no vague references from current news stories to a 17-year-old who had gone missing at a house party. I drummed my fingers against the gray keyboard, biting my lip, and then searched Charlotte's address, pulling up a map that I zoomed in on once, twice, three times. Finally I could make out the outline of her house, sprawling and self-satisfied, and then the green stretch of land that led down from the house to the water.

I saw the two houses on either side of Charlotte's, the northern one a bit closer, small and huddled like some sad kid sister of the Walters' estate. I tried to remember if Charlotte had told me anything about the people who lived there: they didn't have kids, I thought, or else they would have stuck in my mind.

I tracked lower, curser following the jagged line of the lake. The lake itself stretched for miles and miles—Canada was on the other side, my mother said, but oddly enough most people seemed to disagree. It was the subject of some amusing fights in St. Clair, the more baffling because it was something seemingly so easy to check. But it turned out that it depended on the angle you were looking at, the way you defined "across," even the shifting boundaries that the surveyors put on the wildlands across the lake; apparently, it was a stretch of the border that was not neatly defined, an expanse of pinecone forest that Canada and the United States had settled in large part, but not in the finer details. I moved the map now to track the edge of the lake—huge and dark like an ink stain, even on the computer screen— and passed little sprouts of islands and black stretches of water before hovering over the land across, with a faint gray dotted line smearing the forest beyond. CANADA was on one side, written in tight little letters, and UNITED STATES the other.

But even as I zoomed in, the page reloaded, and I cursed softly. The browser brought me back to Charlotte's address, and the zoomed in focus to her large house. I consider tracking back again, but I had wasted ten minutes already, and took a hurried bite of my peanut butter and jelly sandwich before moving the map south, towards the second neighbor of the Walters.

This neighbor was farther—at least half a mile, which seemed almost infinite, when you were walking the Walters' land. The house was large, sprawling, with clean cut lines and wide windows. You could see it driving up to Charlotte's house on her drive, before the land deepened. Indeed, Charlotte's southern neighbor was pressed much closer up against the road, exposed and vulnerable, while the Walters' house was like a fairy castle nestled deep in the woods, at least a mile in from their gate and mailbox.

Charlotte had talked to me about those neighbors, a little bit. A son our age who went to some prep school out of state and returned every summer to smoke weed on the lake and take classes at the nearby community college. I knew without asking that he had had a crush on her; Charlotte said that he used to walk up a couple times a week, to try and catch her outside. She let him, sometimes. She said he was "interesting" and "a little jumpy," but they hadn't dated, not to my knowledge. Still, it wouldn't be the first time Charlotte had kept a secret like that from me—I only found out that she had made out with Jake Kumar three months after it happened, when Mindy had been teasing her. That was back in sophomore year, and Charlotte had given me a half-shrug, a little embarrassed but not too upset at being found out.

"I didn't want you to worry," she had said, which had only made me feel the fool all the more. "You know, I said I'd help—"

"It's fine," I had said, quickly, careful of eavesdroppers. Charlotte knew I had not had my first kiss yet, and that the whole thing (now, by the age of seventeen, something too heavy and uncomfortable to do away with lightly) "stressed me out," sometimes, as she put it. She had told me with full solemnity early sophomore year that she was not going to make out with one more person until she had set me up satisfactorily. Then came weeks of parties where I would be jammed onto the sofa next to a half-drunk guy, who was obviously only there by Charlotte's orders, and I would pop up at the first opportunity like a jack-in-the-box and scuttle away, ashamed and embarrassed.

I could have just told Charlotte to stop, and indeed, eventually I did, but those first few weeks it felt extremely important to me to impress her. To make her think that I was capable of something as daring and careless as making out with a boy on someone's ratty basement sofa, because she thought it was the right solution and she was doing her best to help me. Finally, disgusted with myself and afraid of offending her further, I had told her that I couldn't do it, not like that, and she had apologized for pressuring, and we had never talked about it again. Though apparently, she had still thought I expected her to keep to the whole "no making out before Reese does" plan, which I didn't. Hence, the lying.

There were other things, too—cryptic glances between her and her brother, strange calls she took from her parents, all escalating in the past few months. I pressed as much as a friend ought, but let her have her privacy; none of my business, that's what I always thought. She had given me my space when I dealt with family stuff sometimes, when it would be too embarrassing to let her in on this missed bill or that half-mad family member.

Still…what if something had been going on? With her prep school neighbor… Tim? Ben? And just because I was too afraid of rocking the boat, of trying her patience, I hadn't even bothered to find out. I groaned and leaned forward, knocking my sandwich onto the floor.

Great. There went lunch.

Sighing, I leaned down to pick it up, ducking beneath the cotton white table to snag the pieces and scrape up the worst of the peanut butter, which had oozed out the sides and onto the carpet.

"…super sad," a familiar voice said, around the corner. I heard footsteps pacing towards me and froze. Mindy, I was almost sure of it. "I mean, like, Aiden used to be cool, he was fine last summer, and then—"

The footsteps stopped outside the computer center. I remained frozen beneath the table, not sure where to go, how to calmly pop my head out from under there with my smashed sandwich and pretend to go about my business.

No, more than that: I wanted to hear. What was sad about Aiden?

"It's from when you two dated," another voice said, and I instantly recognized the reedy twang of Melissa Wichstein, soccer co-captain, one of the girls who, at freshman year tryouts, body-slammed me during a two-on-two drill and snorted with laughter when I locked up and fell to my knees, winded. She had been fake nice to me ever since finding out I was Charlotte's friend, but I still hadn't forgiven her that callous elbow, that snigger that showed very clearly she thought herself (accurately, if I was being honest) the superior athlete, the superior competitor, the superior talent.

"That was ages ago," Mindy said, and it took me a second to pull myself out of my daydream and realize she was talking about dating Aiden (dating Aiden! When? How?).

"Yes, but he *never* got over it, obviously," Melissa said. "I mean, he's coming home what, every weekend?"

"Just about. Shhh," Mindy said. I could feel her preening beneath the attention, beneath her friend's words. Was it true? An image flashed in my head of Mindy, short and compact and decidedly cute, with her arm around Aiden's waist. Had they talked at the party? I honestly couldn't remember; if anything, I had wondered why Charlotte hadn't invited her, had been keeping an eye out for strange exchanges between the two of them, not for anything with Aiden. But of course, if Charlotte had deliberately left her co-captain off of the invite list, that was as good a reason as any to suspect that she and Aiden did, in fact, have something going on. That perhaps Charlotte was worried about her brother's wounded feelings.

I shifted slightly beneath the table. My legs were starting to burn, and I needed Melissa and Mindy to move down the hall, so I could come up for air. "It's just so sad," Mindy said. "I mean, I wish he'd talk to me, but obviously he's embarrassed. Maybe I should go over there."

"To his house?"

"Yeah. See how he's doing. Make sure he's okay with all of this."

"That's really nice of you. You're *too* nice, Mindy. And what if he's like, you know, unstable?"

Mindy sighed. "Someone needs to talk to him," she said, and I fake gagged beneath the table. "Otherwise, who knows…"

They moved off, finally. I crawled out from beneath the computer table and hurriedly packed my things away. I wished desperately that I had Aiden's number, just to reach out and give him a head's up, on the off chance that he didn't want to see Mindy. And to be honest, who would want to see an ex in the middle of searching for your missing sister?

But I had never gotten Aiden's number. I could always look him up in the directory when I was home, but the thought of calling the Walters' landline made me vaguely nauseous. Another option would be to wait for my mother to come home and take her car to go visit, but what would that prove? I'd come roaring up the Walters' drive late in the evening, probably after Mindy had made her way there, and have to deal with the haunted gazes of Mr. and Mrs. Walters, the accusatory glare of Aiden.

Or, I thought, I could talk to Mindy. Try and tell her that it wasn't a good idea, with everything going on. But Mindy and I had never been close, and I couldn't see that going over well, either.

But…maybe I did have his number. I opened my phone as I strolled to my next class, scrolling through messages and group texts, mostly from some variation of my mother or Charlotte or my shift lead at the St. Clair library. I found the message I had been looking for, a text from Charlotte about Saturday's party, confirming who was picking up what booze. Riley's number I had; there were three others that were unfamiliar, all guys. I searched them one by one until I found one that was in another group text, from a few months ago, when Charlotte had been sending something about Aiden's going-away party.

It was as close a lead as I was going to get.

Is this Aiden? I texted. And then, because I could imagine that was a text anyone in their right mind would not be eager to answer, added, *It's Reese.*

I tucked the phone away, cheeks blazing. I had always respected my boundaries with Charlotte's family, even her friends. I never wanted her to think I was some sort of social climber, or that I was using her to get to anything, or anyone, that orbited her. But desperate times, and all. I felt my phone buzz fifteen minutes into my English class, but dutifully ignored it until I could slip out to go to the bathroom, aware of the way eyes lingered on me as I left.

Yes. What's up?

Cold, clinical. I wasn't sure if that made it easier or harder—easier, probably.

I was in the library, I began, but deleted it. Too much

detail that he didn't need to know. *I just overheard Mindy saying something about going to see you after school. To see if you were okay? Just giving you a heads up.* I pressed send and felt immediately stupid, after. So what if a girl wanted to go out and comfort him? Maybe they did have something going, and maybe I was really sticking my nose in it. I turned red as I slipped into the blue-tiled bathroom, wondering how something that seemed such a naturally good idea seconds before had turned into something foolish and mortifying.

The response felt like it took ages to come back. I dallied in the bathroom, fiddling with the taps and the soap dispenser, so that if anyone came in it would look like I was just finishing up. Finally, my phone buzzed again.

Ok, thanks.

I flushed again. I should've just left it; of course I should have. None of my business, especially if they had a history. To make matters worse, I was embarrassed over how embarrassed the whole situation made me, and didn't like what it seemed to say about how much I cared about a stranger's opinion. Charlotte wouldn't have; she would have laughed it off, or not given it a second thought.

Or, a voice inside me whispered, *she never would have sent that stupid text to begin with.*

I was almost back to class when my phone buzzed again. I recognized Aiden's number before I opened it.

Do you have plans after school? Need to ask something, about Charlotte.

I hesitated, took the long way back by veering down the wrong hallway. I told him I was free; he suggested I come over around six. It took a few more back-and-forths to establish that I did not have a car, and that he did not want to go anywhere in public and deal with people's questions and stares. Finally Aiden said that he would pick me up at Wolfclaw Coffee, just down the street—a relief, as I didn't need anyone else seeing me get into Aiden's black sports car.

I felt a vague sense of unease that I couldn't place, not until the next bell rang, and I hurried to my last class. The way Aiden had been texting, the fact that he wanted to meet me—it meant that Charlotte still had not been found. That there were no promising new leads eating up his attention. It had almost been forty-eight hours.

CHAPTER 15

*C*harlotte had always been a little obsessed with true crime. It made me feel that somehow, everything that had happened could still be some perverse joke, that she had made some sort of horrible misstep and would emerge from the forest grinning and unharmed, not quite understanding the magnitude of what she had done. Charlotte could be like that, sometimes; people let her get away with a lot, myself included, and as a result, she didn't quite understand normal boundaries.

I couldn't remember where it had started. My thoughts drifted as I doodled on my European History handout, chewing on the inside of my cheek. Ever since I had known Charlotte, she had wanted to watch cop shows and dramas and true crime documentaries. At one point I asked if she wanted to be a detective or a reporter, but that had gone over all wrong—Charlotte had laughed, heartily and long, and said that she couldn't think of a more depressing job than searching for answers that might never be there.

"I'll probably be a doctor," she said, casually, as if that was something she could do on a whim. We had been sixteen, eating buttered popcorn out of metal bowls in her basement, covered with thick woolen blankets in early February. "People like doctors, and they make a lot of money."

I didn't answer—I had a slightly different view of doctors from my mother, who respected and admired some and feverishly despised others that she worked with. *They're humans, too, Reese*, she would tell me, as if I had ever suggested otherwise. *The good ones are good, and the bad ones—well, trust me. You don't want a bad one.*

We had gone back to watching the documentary, then, one about a missing girl whose body had never been found, the camera circling relentlessly between her clean-cut and earnest boyfriend, her well-to-do and slim parents, her best friend, beautiful and wrecked. "You know why they chose this girl to do a documentary about?" Charlotte said, gesturing towards the glowing screen.

"She's rich."

"Rich, beautiful, young," Charlotte said, ticking the traits off on her fingers. "Somehow people think there's something way more tragic about a beautiful young girl dying. The way people care about it so much…it gets creepy, doesn't it?"

"I guess."

"It *is*, because you know that when a pretty young girl goes missing, they're thinking of all the terrible things that could happen to her. That wouldn't happen to someone older, or a boy—at least, probably not."

I had squirmed uncomfortably on the sofa. Charlotte

got like this, sometimes, viciously observant, harsh, eager to talk of the realities of the world in a tone that suggested defiance and even anger. I didn't want to think about the world like that, or to examine why it was we were watching a documentary that was made about a pretty young dead girl rather than one about an equally tragic case.

"I guess it's…potential, too," I said reluctantly. "People just assume someone young and pretty and well-off has more than someone else."

"Exactly," Charlotte said, eyes gleaming. "We just assume that their life is more valuable than other people's. Which is messed up, isn't it?"

"Yes. And also—well. People probably like the schaudenfraude of seeing something bad happen to someone who was probably much luckier than they are."

"Shoi-den-what?"

"Schaudenfraude, like, the enjoyment of seeing bad things happen to other people."

Charlotte gave me a weird look, like I had made the term up. "That's a good point," she said finally. "Like some sort of crazy wish fulfillment."

"Something like that."

Charlotte collapsed once more in her seat, drawing the popcorn bowl back over her spindly legs. "Screw people," she said.

We had heard footsteps at the top of the stairs, then. The door to the basement opened, and Aiden and three of his friends descended halfway down. "Oh," he said, pulling up short when he spotted us. Charlotte turned lazily around and gave her brother a wave; I swiveled around to look at the three football guys and swung quickly back again, pretending to be absorbed in the documentary. "Hey, Charlotte, how much longer will you be? The guys want to play some video games."

"Forty minutes," she said, checking the time left on the show.

"Ah, come on, Charlotte, I know you'd rather shoot aliens with us," one of the guys said. Jack? Jared? A guy who had, more than once, stopped by our lunch table at school to chat with Charlotte, making casual conversation about an upcoming game, or dropping hints about a school dance.

"No, thanks."

The guy strolled over to the couch, pressing his arms against the back of the sofa. "Depressing," he said, after a few seconds. "Hey, Aiden, where's the television plug? I say we take this room by force."

"Let them finish," Aiden said. "Let's get some food."

Charlotte rolled her eyes at me as Jack/Jared finally left, clambering up the long stairs. She passed the popcorn bowl back to me, and we settled in to watch the rest of the documentary: the crafted interviews, the gray and green panoramas of the sleepy Oregon town, the reenactments, comedic but also slightly sickening, driving home that here was death laid out for our entertainment, tragedy sacrificed to the altar of a show.

CHAPTER 16

I hurried to Wolfclaw as soon as the final bell rang, as much for coffee as to minimize the time that Aiden's car was conspicuously waiting outside— and the number of eyes who saw me get into it.

The café was just starting to build to its after-school buzz when I arrived. The coffee shop was nestled between two nostalgic shops, so nestled into the past they verged on parody: a record shop on one side, glistening and retro, and a camera film shop on the other, where you could rent giant old cameras for a week if you had a fake I.D. or a sibling over eighteen willing to spot you for it.

The coffee shop itself was the type that was overly cool to the point of being obnoxious, with a chalkboard wall on one side containing illustrated graphics of giant coffee machines with intricate pipes and levers and churning espresso beans, and a brick wall on the other side, check-ered with hanging charcoal drawings of spots around St. Clair. The menu itself was drawn in chalk behind the main counter, and pastries were displayed on open little plates with gluten-free and vegan labels written in black-sharpie calligraphy on colorful paper. The café was sustainable through and through, which meant essentially that they did not do to-go cups unless you brought your own, and instead of plastic straws they would hand you a little metal spoon to hold back the ice as you drank, and a couple napkins when this strategy inevitably failed.

The bar was staffed today by a scraggly, bald, tattooed barista with a bristly ginger beard reaching nearly to his chest and a brown-skinned girl with purple and green hair and two lip piercings who wore large fake frames when it suited her and—summer or winter—always had on some variation of fishnet stockings, boots, and a black top. I think the whole town felt proud to have something of the city "hipness" infused into our little corner of St. Clair— usually such coffee shops and the people who inhabited them stayed within the confines of the city, ten miles south and west. But I wondered, as I ordered a lavender latte and handed over my thermos, if the people working there felt the same way. I had always taken their scowling faces and judgmental peering over our pressing of the "tip" buttons as more local character—the cranky city hipsters, scornful and too cool, come to perform for us and show us just how awful we might be if we grew up outside of our neighbor-hood bubble.

I moved to the bar to wait, climbing up onto one of the black stools where you could watch the baristas steaming and frothing and pouring and grinding. Perhaps they didn't like us because we were a bunch of high schoolers, giggling and indecisive and too concerned with what each other thought to be really and truly courteous. Or perhaps it was something even simpler than that—their commute was too long, the café paid horribly, high schoolers were not the best tippers. I thought, for a moment, about how my perception of people was often so morbidly centered around myself, each person's moods and eccentricities judged as if they were somehow in response to or anticipation of something I did or would do. We were all working off of partial information about people around us—sometimes about the people closest to us. And that messed up everything, made you think that a short text message was about some hidden slight, made you believe that a girl's cold shoulder was personal instead of drawn from hurt, made you think that your friend's inconsistencies were due to something you did or said, rather than…than…

"Latte for Reese," the female barista said, handing over my thermos with a sigh, fingers barely touching the turquoise shell as if the color or shape of it offended her. I muttered my thanks and left the shop to hover outside, feeling like I was swimming up from some hidden depth of thoughts to break the surface. Charlotte had been acting odd, these past couple of weeks. She would flake suddenly, or would be moody and untalkative other times. I assumed it was something I had said, bringing up college applications or asking about field hockey matches—probably things her parents were giving her hassle about. But what if it wasn't? What if something else was going on?

Aiden roared down the street just as I stepped outside. Kids stopped to stare, coffee cups and books clutched in their hands. He pulled up to the side and cut the engine, leaving a pregnant, empty silence behind.

"Hey," I said, slipping as quickly as possible into the

passenger seat. The inside was all black leather and faux wood, the seat much too low to be comfortable. In fact I hated Aiden's car, privately agreeing with Charlotte that it was an awful, narrow bug of a thing, fast and sleek but uncomfortable and sharp-edged. "Only son," she would say, lifting one wry eyebrow at the thing. "My mom can't say no to him."

"Ah, I miss that place," Aiden said, by way of response, eyes darting towards my thermos as the scent of espresso filled the car.

"Want some?"

I had meant it only as a courtesy, but Aiden accepted the thermos and took a tiny sip from it, sighing. "We can stop and get you one," I said, amused (and not a little surprised that Aiden Walters would deign to share a thermos full of latte with anyone, let alone me—Charlotte had always said he was a germaphobe).

"Nah, I'm good. I'll make one at home." He seemed to notice the eyes upon us, and deftly put the car in gear. We roared down the lane, me closing my thermos with a frantic motion as my shoulders were thrown back against the seat.

"Sorry," Aiden said, with a ghost of a grin. "I forget, about the pick up."

But he sobered as we drove farther and farther from the school and closer to his home. I was grateful he didn't want to talk; the quick motion of the car made me nauseous, and I found myself missing Charlotte's large SUV and her careful, slow movements. Aiden, at some point, seemed to notice, and slowed down enough that I could manage to actually take a sip of my latte. We didn't discuss Mindy, nor Charlotte, nor any of the awfulness swirling around us; we just drove, in strangely comforting silence, until we pulled through the stone gates and rolled up the drive to the front door.

I tensed. It was stupid, but I hadn't even thought of the fact that I would be seeing Mr. and Mrs. Walters until I spotted their cars in the long, circular drive. My panic must have showed, for Aiden said, "Don't worry. We'll go upstairs."

"I'm not worried," I lied. I climbed out of the low car and onto the gravel drive, heart fluttering in my chest. Aiden locked it and strode ahead of me, past the neatly clipped hedges and over the pink stone walkway to the grand double-door entry that had always reminded me of some fairy-tale fortress.

"If you say 'fairy-tale' one more time about this house," Charlotte used to say to me, rolling her eyes.

But it was. I felt like I was seeing it afresh, sans Charlotte. Double-story entryway, spiral staircase extending off both sides, and then, once you went into the kitchen and living area, everything suddenly became sleek and steel and modern, with large bay windows on one side and kitchen appliances that looked like they belonged in a spaceship on the other. The fridge was made to look like cabinets; the microwave was made to look like just another drawer. The stove heated food with protons or electrons or neutrons or something, and the double oven had about twenty buttons, five of which were required to even get the thing on. When I had first come, I had marveled at how at-home Charlotte was in all of it, as if she had been tailor-made in the same way as the house: beautiful, complicated, baffling. The mystery had worn away a little, over the years, but it struck me now afresh.

I heard footsteps on the back stairs and tensed. Aiden grabbed a water bottle from the fridge and motioned me forwards, towards the entryway staircase, but we had no sooner gotten a few steps up than Mrs. Walters stepped out, slim and bare-faced in a pair of slacks and a sweater, and looked up at me.

Haunted. That was the best way to describe her. Her face was pale, features pinched, and her eyes had dark shadows rimmed in red. She was still beautiful, even without makeup, and her face was smooth and taut. Her hands fluttered in front of her, half-reaching for me.

"Reese."

It was like a summons from a ghost; I went to her.

"Mom, we're just going to go through some of Charlotte's stuff. See if the detectives missed something," Aiden said.

"Would Charlotte like that?" Mrs. Walters said sharply, embracing me with bird-thin wrists as her face tilted to her son over my shoulder. She felt so weak, so light. I marveled at the change that could take place in just a day, like a curse. Mrs. Walters had always been elegant, ethereal, but she was fragile now, too. Withering away.

"I think she'd like anything that would help us find her," Aiden replied, and the air was sharp, tense.

"We won't touch anything we shouldn't," I promised Mrs. Walters. "I'll make sure."

She glanced back at me, not quite seeing me, even as her hand lifted to press against my cheek. She had always liked me, I thought, especially once it became apparent that I wasn't going anywhere. I found out a year or so ago that Mrs. Walters had always asked me to come on family vacations, but Charlotte, embarrassed, had always declined on my behalf. "You'd hate them," she told me later. "Ski lodges or cruises or awful European hotels that Dad picks out because they look 'quaint.' They make us go to museums or take lessons or do other 'enriching activities.'" I had laughed with her, pretending I would have hated it, trying to hide how much I envied the family for spending time together, for having rituals and traditions that were just theirs. I had not seen my father for fifteen years; my mother said he had remarried, but neither of us had any inclination to look him up. The child support checks he had used to send had hardly been worth the pursuit, when they finally stopped—my mother had mentioned that often enough, dropping hints about "good lawyers."

"We're going to find her," Mrs. Walters now said to me. It was almost a question.

"We will," I said urgently. Of course we would. She smiled faintly.

"Go sit down, Mom, rest," Aiden said, descending another stair. "We'll come get you if we find anything."

"Rest," she said. "Yes—yes, that's a good idea." She floated off, looking a bit lost as she rounded the corner of the house, sending one more mournful glance up at Aiden.

"Alright," Aiden said. Something tight was in his voice, something I couldn't recognize. "Let's go."

"Do you really want to search Charlotte's rooms?" I said. "I thought you had something to ask me, about her."

"I do. But we're going to search her rooms first." Aiden shot a glance back at me as we arrived at the landing, defiant, daring me to challenge him. I stayed silent. "I know my sister has been hiding something, these past few months. I've assumed you've noticed, or she's told you?" His lips twitched at my blank stare. "No, I guess not. Well. Surprising. I guess it means that it's that much more important to find out what exactly it is."

CHAPTER 17

"*Hiding* something?" I repeated, as Aiden ducked down the hall and to the heavy white door that led to Charlotte's room. "What do you mean?"

"I don't know what. But I know my sister. She's been... a little off. Even more than she should be with—well." He pushed open the door, revealing Charlotte's room beyond.

The room was wide and bright, with its own en suite bathroom. It was strange to see it in the slanting afternoon fall light, bed still made, homework still splayed out across the oak desk facing wide double-windows that looked over the lawn. It looked simultaneously like Charlotte had not stepped inside in years, and like Charlotte would return any moment, a fay entering some preserved dream.

But even as I looked, I noticed little details that were off: on second glance, the homework was not splayed across the desk, but arranged in neat little nonsensical stacks: binders on one side, notebooks on another, pens gathered together at the top of the desk. Her laptop was nowhere to be found. The curtains were drawn back all the way, which was never the case—Charlotte usually tucked the curtains just a foot or so open, enough for a view, not enough to send blazing light into the white, cream, and blue room. Her trash was all empty, no new bag, nothing, just gaping holes in the patterned metal tins that were arranged near her bed and beneath her desk.

"Yeah," Aiden said, his eyes slicing right towards me. "You can tell, can't you? Even though they cleaned it up."

"Who…?" Chills raced up my spine.

"The police," Aiden said. "Who did you think?"

"Oh, right. Police." And then, "Why?"

"Well, in case of foul play." His lips curled around the words, and I felt a stab of panic. The concept itself didn't surprise me, but the idea that the police had already jumped there… Had they found something else, some other evidence out there, that night?

"What were they looking for?"

"Oh, they weren't going to tell us. Suspects, and all. Relax," he said, seeing my expression. "Everyone's a suspect, right now."

Which meant me as well. I felt another wave of heat go through me. It was fine—it was all going to be fine. Charlotte would turn up soon, anyway, and then all of this would go away. When Charlotte returned, unharmed and safe.

"Okay," Aiden said, scanning the room. "You're up. I looked before the police came, and I couldn't find anything suspicious. But I'm guessing if there are any special places where Charlotte hides something…"

An image leaped into my mind, but I pressed my lips

shut. "You'll have to give me an idea of what I'm looking for."

The silence stretched between us; we still hadn't flicked a bedroom light on, and in the late afternoon the whole room took on an orange cast, shadows twisted and lengthened. When I glanced at Aiden, he seemed taller, stretched, like some ghoul or monstrous fairy. I took a step back and turned on the overhead light, sending fractured white light spilling across the room. Aiden blinked; the illusion was gone.

"Well," Aiden said. "I don't know, not exactly. But maybe—something about Danny, maybe."

"Danny?" That was a surprise.

Aiden seemed to notice my tone. "Yeah," he said. "There's something... She's been talking to him more recently, on the phone. Were they dating?"

"No, of course not." My mind spun; were they? Would Charlotte hide something like that from me? "She wouldn't —I don't think so."

Aiden let the silence hang in the air, gaze locked on me. I shook my head. I wouldn't hide that, not now, not if it could be important. "What were they talking about?" I said finally.

I saw him search my face; then, he must have decided I was telling the truth, or close enough to it, for he said, "I don't know. I saw his name on her phone a couple of times. She'd take it upstairs. I thought maybe, you know..." He shrugged. "Why else talk to him all the time?"

Danny. No, that couldn't be. He was barely a blip on the radar for Charlotte. In fact, she hadn't seemed interested at all this fall in talking to boys: instead, there were college applications, interviews, all sorts of things to worry about. And a strange reticence; yes, I had noticed that, but certainly it couldn't be because she was hiding some secret romance.

"I don't know," I said finally, embarrassed to admit it. "She didn't tell me anything about that." I broke away from Aiden's gaze and stepped into the room. There, I couldn't be any help. But in searching, perhaps...

I walked forward, checking under the mattress first. It was a kid's hiding spot, obvious and silly, but Charlotte and I had hidden little notebooks and letters beneath there in middle school, swearing we would only unearth them at college graduation, to see if our predictions had come true.

"Police tried that," Aiden said, crossing his arms and leaning up against the door frame. "First thing I saw, before they told me kindly to get lost."

"Right," I said. My hands came up empty. I moved to the bottom of the bed, to the little slit in the mattress where we had hidden some of our more sensitive letters. Mattress springs poked my fingers as I dug them into the soft stuffing, pulling out a handful of letters with our middle-school scrawl. Aiden looked duly impressed.

"Let's see those here," he said, stepping closer.

"It's not related." I sorted through the letters. "We wrote these when we were kids. If there's nothing else in here—"

There wasn't. I didn't let Aiden see the letters, which he protested at first, but came around to quickly enough. I moved farther into the room.

The toilet tank had been duly searched and cleaned;

I hadn't expected to find anything there, but Charlotte and I had once joked, during a true crime show, that it would be a great place to hide a weapon. Her sock drawer was similarly clean, except for the wad of cash that had been tucked into the same back corner where Charlotte always kept it. I tapped my fingers on my thigh, spinning around the small room, eyes darting from the lacy cream lamp shades to the bamboo stalks plunged into glass marbles on her bedside to the family portrait, grim and haunting, on the wall opposite the bright windows. I picked the last up, looked behind it, and Aiden snorted.

"Looking for a hidden vault?" he said. "There is one, you know. Just not in Charlotte's room. My mom has a fondness for secret doors and such."

I didn't say anything. I moved to the bookcase, finally, a long shelf of leather-bound classics that, to my knowledge, Charlotte had never touched. My fingers moved along the spines, touching the pages absently, trying to wrack my brain. If I were Charlotte, where would I hide something? But more important, more integral to that question, seemed to be what I would hide. My mind spun; it kept coming up blank.

I froze. Aiden had lost interest in my wanderings; he had begun searching through Charlotte's desk instead, pulling open drawers and rifling through papers and old chargers. My fingers twitched back to the last book they had run over, one that blended in with all the rest but that felt lighter, more plastic. I glanced at the spine. *A Tale of Two Cities* by Charles Dickens. That was a small book, wasn't it? We had read it sophomore year, and it had been a slim little paperback, not this hulking volume in front of me. I yanked it out.

I heard the thud and rattle as I moved to cradle the book in my hands. From there, it was as simple as pulling open the cover, which revealed not the words of some old white man but a cavernous interior, filled with a mess of wires.

I began to untangle them, setting the book on the shelf as Aiden continued to shuffle papers behind me. At the end of one of the wires I saw a black sphere—no, a microphone. I raised it to my eye, pressing on the hard tip of it with one finger.

"The police," Aiden said behind me, sounding frustrated as he pulled open yet another drawer, "have been just about as helpful as you'd expect. Acting cagey, like maybe *we* had something to do with it, not answering a single question my dad asked, telling my mom that they're pursuing 'all angles,' as if that's supposed to mean anything to us…" He slammed the drawer closed, whipping around towards me.

"What's that?" he said, tone changed.

I held it out to him.

He moved to me like a predator, quick and intense, and as I handed him the microphone I had a flash of memory of a different Aiden, the one who had sat by my bedside the night Charlotte went missing, pale and sunken and withdrawn, hand reaching out towards mine. I wondered, with momentary dizziness, if I had wholly imagined that night. Certainly Aiden seemed to take care not to touch me at all as he unwound the wire from my hands.

"What's this from?" he said harshly.

"I don't know."

"How did you find it?"

I pointed to the hollow book. He frowned, measured its weight in his hand, and began rifling through the others. I turned to help; in another few minutes' search, we had found one more, on the bottom shelf, this one with an even greater mess of wires and black boxes and little rolls of black tape. "What the actual," Aiden began, under his breath.

The door to the room swung open.

We jumped like guilty criminals; Aiden even stuffed the whole book behind his back, swinging around to face the intruder. I turned, a little more slowly, pretending to adjust a picture of Charlotte as I did so.

Mr. Walters.

He looked too haunted to have seen what we were doing, let alone care enough to ask. I almost gasped at the sight of him. Never had I seen Charlotte's dad look so sunken, so collapsed in upon himself. It was like Mrs. Walters again, but ten times worse: his brown hair had thinned and turned half-gray, and his broad shoulders were stooped and fragile. He must have lost, since I had last seen him (weeks? Months ago? Why couldn't I remember?) at least twenty pounds. Could that really happen to someone just within a few days?

He didn't even acknowledge me. "Divers," he croaked, towards Aiden. It took him three tries for the word to be intelligible. "They've brought divers, to the lake. To look for her."

I couldn't help it. My eyes wandered towards the open windows, towards the vast expanse of forest that ended somewhere in the dark, murky water. I thought of the rowboat, of the blanket, of the dark figure with a hood pulled low over its head.

No, I thought, and my heart began to race. Not like this. We couldn't find her like this.

CHAPTER 18

*J*called my mom to pick me up, not able to stand the idea of waiting in the kitchen with Charlotte's parents and brother, like some interloper bearing witness to their grief. Aiden's sharp gaze told me that we'd discuss the recording devices later; I tried, probably without success, to nod and indicate that I understood.

My mother, to her credit, came immediately, and didn't even question what I had been up to as we drove home. Instead she reached out and squeezed my forearm. "If there's anything I can do," she said, "you let me know."

I went home that night and texted Charlotte, even though I knew her phone was dead, even though presumably the police had not been able to triangulate its location using whatever high-tech toys they had on hand. *We'll find you*, I said. I watched for a few seconds, waiting for the typing bubble to appear. In the dim glow of my nightlight, covers pulled high over my shoulders, moonlight spilling through the gauzy curtains of my cramped room, it seemed like it could be possible. It seemed like someone, something, would text me back.

I breathed into my sheets, eyes focused on my phone. I could still smell the rosemary from my mother's cooking, baby potatoes and sausages that had been oiled and dressed and dusted with spices before being shoved in the oven while my mother hurried to finish up whatever other chores she had before collapsing in bed or running out to the next shift. Usually something ended up burnt, but at least it had been a few years since we had set off the smoke alarms—I had gotten my mom to promise to only cook when I was in the house, and I had gotten in the habit of checking the stove every fifteen minutes.

As I waited the temperature in the room seemed to slowly drop, and I thought of the coming winter: of metal telephone poles coated with ice or cars buried under mounds of freshly fallen snow. I thought too about a movie I had watched once with Charlotte, that said a cold room was a sign that ghosts were nearby. Goosebumps raced up my arm. I set the phone down and checked the clock. Quarter to midnight.

The phone chimed.

My pulse quickened. I considered, for a moment, ducking under my sheets and curling my body into a little ball, no fingers or toes over the sides of the bed, all parts of me safe beneath the covers, like I did when I was a little kid and was afraid that monsters would snatch me off the mattress if I had even the tiniest bit exposed. But then, before I could let the fear catch up to me anymore, I snaked my hand out and picked up the phone.

One text message.

From Riley Gallagher.

I half-laughed, giddy with relief. A real human, not some ghost. Charlotte was all right, she had to be all right, but her phone was out of commission, and she would not text me back.

I'd have to find her another way.

I opened Riley's text, figuring I could respond in the morning, when normal humans were expected to be communicating.

It was long—a whole paragraph. My fear of ghosts evaporated, replaced by a baffled curiosity. My hand hovered over the lock and home button, ready to take a screenshot and send to Charlotte, muscle memory not quite caught up with my brain. I reread it once, twice:

Hey, just wanted to say, sorry I got involved at all this morning. Not my business what you want to do or who you want to see. Was just being paranoid. See you around.

The tone was curt, clipped. Or was I imagining it? I didn't text enough boys to know how they usually spoke. I considered replying right then and there, but instinct held me back: I felt sure that if I broke and texted now, revealing I was up, Riley would leave me hanging until the morning, and I didn't want to give up that silly junior high upper hand.

I was being dismissed, somehow. Why?

Maybe he had seen me get into Aiden's car that afternoon, after his warning to me. But then, so what? I could do what I wanted, for my own reasons. And if he couldn't give me his, then why would I listen to them?

But why withdraw the warning, once he saw I wasn't heeding it? Why not just explain things to me?

See you around. That part, I thought, was the effective dismissal. The acknowledgement that any disclosures on his part had come to an end, as if I had failed some silly little test.

It didn't matter. Whatever he was hiding, if it related to Charlotte, I'd find it out. I thought of the divers, pirouetting in the lake, fingers outstretched towards dark sediment, bodies twisting through the upended dirt. They hadn't found anything—they couldn't have, or Aiden would have told me. Wouldn't he?

I shivered and pulled the covers higher over my head.

I had a feeling, even then, that I was wrong.

CHAPTER 19

*W*hen I emerged from my bedroom the next morning, Aiden's car was outside. My mother sat at the front window, hands curled around her coffee cup, laptop open, scrubs on, Morty lying quietly by her feet. Her wavy hair was pulled back into a high, tight ponytail, and her eyes were fixed on the unmoving car as she took another delicate sip from her mug.

"What does he want?" my mother said as I walked in and froze, taking in the scene. "It can't be about Charlotte. Nothing on the news, yet."

"I-I don't know."

My mother frowned. In the morning light she looked young, like an older sister instead of a parent. Her eyes drifted slowly to me. "Did he have anything to do with what happened?"

I blinked. I wanted to act outraged, to shout, *Why would you even think that?* and *What kind of question is that?* But instead I said the truth.

"I don't know."

My mother nodded. "You be careful, Reese. Until they know what happened."

"I will."

"No, really." My mother closed her laptop and turned the full force of her gaze on me. "The police are looking for suspects."

"They don't even know what happened yet."

"Still. For when they do." She waved her hand, as if the fate of Charlotte—*missing, kidnapped, murdered*—was irrelevant, inconsequential. "If someone did something that night, then that means you all were at risk, you understand? You might have seen something, or know something, that someone doesn't want you to know."

I felt the hairs on the back of my neck begin to stand up. I began to protest, but my mother cut me off again.

"Just promise me you'll be careful. You're a smart girl." She jerked her thumb at the car out front. "Do you think he had anything to do with it?"

I took a deep breath, allowing my brain to calculate in the interim. "No," I said on exhale, and I was surprised at how much it rang true. No, in my heart of hearts, I did not think Aiden had anything to do with Charlotte's disappearance.

It didn't mean, of course, that he didn't have other things to hide.

She nodded, seemingly satisfied. "Okay." She took a breath. "Don't leave without breakfast."

I obligingly took an oat bar out of the pantry and waved good-bye. We both knew without a discussion that Aiden would drive me to school. That was one thing I liked about my mother—not every little thing was a negotiation, a power struggle, like it could sometimes be with Charlotte and her family. Get an A in this class or else no car, do this chore or else we won't get takeout for dinner tonight. Little things, things that made sense individually but that piled up all together felt like a nonsensical maze designed to trap and smother.

My mother caught me by the arm as I left and pulled me into a rare hug. It was brief, quick, bony: at forty-five, my mother was already frail and a little hunched, her blonde hair streaked with gray. And then it was over, and we both said I love you without looking at each other, and I stepped out into the November morning and strode up to Aiden's idling car, a pit sinking deeper and deeper into my stomach.

CHAPTER 20

"They're sure it's her phone?"

Aiden nodded, once. He had been cold since I had climbed inside, only offering mechanically to take me as far as the cross-streets two blocks before the school, to avoid the worst of the traffic. And then he had explained, robot-like and pale, that Charlotte's phone had been found at the bottom of the lake.

I could feel him sneaking glances at me whenever we came to a red light, but when I looked back at Aiden he jerked his head away, jaw clenched, eyes scrunched in something like fear or fury or both. "What...what do the police think happened?" I said.

It was apparently the wrong thing to say, for I saw Aiden's jaw tighten, and he cut another quick glance sideways at me. "They don't know. Any theories?"

"No. I mean...the rowboat..." I thought again of the hooded figure, the oars dipping in and out of the water, the moonlight illuminating that bundle at the front of the boat.

"They haven't found any sign of the rowboat."

"It's a big lake," I said, though my throat had tightened, and I feared that he could hear the worry in my voice. I cleared it and tried again. "They still have time. They'll find her."

"Will they?"

"What do you mean?" I said. My mother's warning pounded in my ears; suddenly I was very aware that we were alone, that Aiden could take me anywhere he wanted, and no one would know for hours, maybe the whole day. I tried to glance out the window to catch a street sign, make sure we were on the right path, but I never paid attention to directions and the streets were whipping by too quickly to make out any of their names. I had been so sure that Aiden had had nothing to do with Charlotte's murder, but that had been the Aiden of yesterday, quiet and reserved, or the Aiden of Saturday night, needy and distraught. This Aiden—cold and furious—I didn't know.

"I mean," Aiden said, taking a sharp right, so fast that my seatbelt tightened against my chest, "that if you saw anything else that night, now is as good a time as any to talk about it."

"What?"

Aiden cut the radio, which had been playing, so faint as to be almost imperceptible, some old jazz tunes. "I said that if you saw anything else that night—"

"I heard you. I just don't know what you mean. Anything else?"

He gave me a withering look. I shrank away, embarrassed and furious all at once. What did I do?

"You were the last one to see her," Aiden said quietly. "You were the only one out there when—"

"Pull over."

"Just tell me." Aiden's fingers drummed on the steering wheel, his face white, making his blue eyes seem even brighter, almost feverish. "If that night, when I came—if there was something else you knew, something that—" His words became tighter and more forceful, and finally he stopped, shaking his head.

We slowed and then stopped at a red light. I unclipped my seatbelt and opened the door.

"Hey!" Aiden said, reaching out at the empty space I left behind as I deftly maneuvered out of the car. "Reese, wait. This isn't a game. I need to know."

"I'm not hiding anything. I didn't—I wasn't—" I couldn't bring myself to even say the words. *I had nothing to do with your sister disappearing.* It came as a slap in the face to think that Aiden, who had been with me most of the night, could think that. It meant that others had, too—perhaps the police. A jolt of self-preservation went through me, adrenaline driving out some of the numbness. I had to get away. Had to think.

Aiden rolled down the window. "Let me drive you closer, at least," he said, as the light flicked green. Someone behind him honked.

I waved him forward and stepped onto the sidewalk. After another ten seconds—and three more increasingly long honks—he gave up and sped off.

CHAPTER 21

*T*he thing was, it had become more and more clear to me over the past few weeks that something had been wrong with Charlotte. But I had chosen not to see.

Instead, I had wanted Charlotte to be the person she had always been for me: confident, daring, carefree. The way she had seemed that night at the party, when she had flashed back to her mischievous self. Now I wondered if that was another sign something had gone wrong.

What if I had stopped and asked her to talk to me, demanded that she let me know what was on her mind the way she did for me sometimes? I just was so unused to that role with Charlotte—in my mind, she had always been the perfect one, and I had been the one tagging along, the only one to need help. So much so that when she might have actually needed help of her own, I had been too blind or too unwilling to see it.

As I trudged the last mile towards school, I thought back to the first week of classes that year, when Charlotte and I had taken our fresh books and bulging bags out to the lakeshore, spreading them out on a picnic table as the end-of-summer breeze whipped around us. We were both in outfits picked carefully out for the first of the year, mine a black skirt and ruffled peasant top, hers a simple black dress ornamented with oversized pearls and clunky gold jewelry. She looked, with her sunglasses on, like an old-style movie star.

After a couple of failed probes, I knew better than to ask about college applications or plans for next year. I had assumed that she had just procrastinated over the summer, like most of the rest of the school, and didn't want to be reminded of it.

Instead, we looked out in silence over the water, inhaling the scent of grass and damp wood, listening to the buzz of flies and the gentle lap of waves. I watched them, hypnotized, thinking how surprised I had been to see waves in a lake when I first moved to St. Clair. Nothing like the crash of ocean against rocks or sandy beaches: these were gentle waves, little tentative laps, peaceful and sooth-ing. Soon, the whole lake would be frozen over, life suspended for a few months under layers of crystalline ice.

"What do you think," Charlotte had asked, lazily, casu-ally, and I braced for it: the name of some guy she was interested in, the name of some couple that baffled her, the name of a teacher who would become her personal enemy for that year. "What do you think it's like to die?"

I jerked my neck left, so sharply that I nearly fell off the seat. "What?" I said, sure that I had not heard correctly.

Charlotte's sunglasses were still on. Her face was unreadable. "What do you think it's like to die?"

I searched her still, trying to see any hint of what she meant. "Have you been watching a crime show?" I said.

A small smile. "Not lately."

I blinked. "Well," I said, "is—I mean is—"

"Oh, don't worry," Charlotte said, with a short laugh. She kicked up her legs on the picnic table and leaned back. "I'm not going through an emo phase, or anything. I was just wondering."

Probably peaceful, I almost said. Because the topic—or rather, Charlotte's attitude about it—was giving me the creeps, even on the bright, sunlit day. We both loved true crime and crime shows, sure, but that was because, to my mind, those stories were always so remote, with that scintillating sense that it *could* happen here, but certainly it *wouldn't*.

"I think," I said carefully. "Honestly? Hard. Slow."

"You're talking about aging."

"Isn't that what you're talking about?"

She considered. "Yes," she said. "Yes, it is."

We sat in silence for a minute longer. I thought about the only person I had ever really seen, up close, go through the phase of dying—there wasn't a more elegant way to put it. My Uncle Richard, down in Florida, who had sent me Christmas cards and occasionally, at my mother's insistence, called me on the phone to talk. He had pancreatic cancer, and went from a healthy sixty-five-year-old with some stomach pain to a cancer patient in the spate of a few months. Even now, I still couldn't shake the sense that it was the hospital that had made him sick, with its endless appointments and pokings and proddings, the port that went right into his chest where the chemo drip went. They gave him six months, and he lived eighteen—if you could call it that. The chemo stole half of his days from him; the other half he moved around like a zombie, with pained smiles and long sighs, looking forward mostly to his naps. My mother and I had flown down every three months to spend a week with him, and it shocked me how much the disease or the medicine or both stole. Sometimes he would try to ask about how school was for me, or how my mom's job was. Other times, the times when he would light up, we would talk about his childhood with my mom out in Cleveland, trips to the lakeshore, marshmallows by the fire when they went camping.

Many times, he would want to talk about death. How fast it was coming, if the chemo was doing anything at all. I would put on a blindly optimistic face and tell him that I thought he was so much better, that I could see the improvement—he would smile, but it had always haunted me, after, that I had not said the right thing. Sometimes I wondered if he had just wanted someone who would let him talk plainly about what was being taken from him, the way my mom did, when she was around. It had been a wonder, actually: she chatted survival charts and chemo side effects with him like they were discussing the daily weather, took him to church every Sunday (none of us, not even my uncle, had gone to more than a Christmas or Easter service in years), and when the time came she mentioned hospice, after which it seemed for a few months like Uncle Richard was making a miracle recovery—before the cancer took him in the end.

It made me think that sometimes, dying young was not so bad: not in the morbid, take a risk and live life sort of way, but just that, if someone served in the army, or had a terrible accident…well, at least they were spared a lot of suffering. A lot of joy, yes, but also a lot of suffering.

I didn't say any of this to Charlotte. Instead I thought about my mother, her thinness that had never left after Uncle Richard's death, her movements slowing, the possible diagnosis that would one day rip her from the world of the healthy into the tornado of hospital visits and treatments that would take her from me.

"I don't want to die," Charlotte said quietly.

I glanced sideways at her. "Are you…not feeling well?" An image flashed into my mind: Charlotte with some sort of eighteenth-century consumptive illness, wasting away in that beautiful and otherworldly way that would make her into something like a psychic or a profit.

"No. God, no." She shook herself. "Still, it's inevitable, right? One day, sooner or later…"

Charlotte's grandmother had died that summer, at the age of eighty-four. I tried not to point out that Charlotte was over sixty years away from that. Instead I said, using one of the hospice nurse's special questions, "What are you afraid of? Specifically."

Charlotte cocked her head sideways. A gust of wind blew her hair over her cheek, and the lock fluttered and came to a rest tucked gently beneath her chin. "Not death itself, exactly—I mean, we're Catholic, so presumably there's something horribly good or horribly bad on the other side of that, but…" She shrugged. "Just the idea that it's so *unfair*."

"That we have to die?"

"No. That some people die in bed surrounded by

family after living a long and successful life. And some people—most people—don't." She pulled her feet off the picnic table and straightened. "*Everything* about it is unfair."

I considered. "Yeah," I said. "That's true." And also a problem for future me, when I wasn't seventeen and worried about college applications and first boyfriends and making a fool of myself at senior presentation.

Charlotte shrugged again, a sour half-smile crossing her face. "Anyway. I suppose there's no getting out of it."

"No. But you can choose how—well, like my uncle," I said, embarrassed. "He didn't choose cancer, but he chose the treatment. And chose when to stop it." Charlotte lifted her chin towards me, face inscrutable. "So you do get to choose some of that. Even when the doctors are, well, a little pushy." Uncle Richard's had not been pleased about the cessation of chemo; my uncle's markers had all been pretty good, apparently, and the oncologist had berated my uncle that he could have at least another year, if he didn't "give up." My mother had put a stop to that, and also filed a formal complaint with the hospital.

"Choose how," Charlotte echoed, mouth moving like she was tasting the words. "Yes—yes, I suppose that's true." We sat in silence for a minute longer, me drowned in memories of Uncle Richard, of the funeral, of the emptiness I had not known had been filled until he died. "Hey," Charlotte said, reaching out to squeeze my arm. "Thanks."

"For what?"

Charlotte smiled. "Tell you more later."

We hadn't spoken of it again.

CHAPTER 22

*B*y the time I arrived at school, I was already ten minutes late. I hurried inside, past the bored glance of the security guard, and into the student center. I slowed as I made my way towards my house: what, honestly, was the point of striding into the middle of Spanish, and possibly being forced to explain myself in a foreign language in front of twenty kids? I turned on my heel and made for the library. I could explain the cut later to my mom; it would be the first one in four years, and I had a feeling that, with everything else going on, she'd help me take care of it.

I went to the back of the media center again, pulling up Charlotte's house on a map. I scrolled down to her southern neighbor, the one she had been so cagey about last year, and scribbled down the address. It couldn't hurt —at the very least, he might be able to tell me if he and Charlotte had ever taken the rowboat out. If he knew where it was kept.

I searched the news right after, trying to find out

anything I could about the investigation. The articles about Charlotte's disappearance were surprisingly scarce; perhaps the police were following a lead and didn't want anything to get out until they finished. Or maybe not. I had no idea how it worked.

The latest article was a two-paragraph post about police's "continuing efforts to find the missing student Charlotte Walters, 17," one paragraph of which was devoted entirely to a description of how to contact the police or use the hotline to leave a tip. I drummed my fingers against the computer, thinking.

I pulled up the map again. Leaning closer, I typed in the neighbor's address, zoomed in. Following the line with my finger, I traced the distance up to the little boathouse where the rowboat was stored. How far was it—one mile, two? I squinted at the key in the bottom right and began to use my thumb as a ruler.

"Computer pass?"

I jumped, glancing right as a long-nosed librarian peered around the corner. Computer passes were required for all blocks except lunch, and I glanced from my screen to her trying to come up with some suitable excuse.

"Um," I said finally, "no?"

After some negotiation, and, I think, recognition on the part of the librarian that I was the missing girl's best friend, I made my way out of the computer lab without a cut slip, off to go down to the student center where students whose parents could afford to get them laptops (read: practically everyone else in St. Clair) sat working away or chatting or wasting time until the next class. I could still feel eyes pulled to me like I was some sort of freakish magnet, whispers cascading behind me. It had been years since the school had had something this exciting happen, and I found myself resenting all of their curious stares, their hungry gazes, their searching looks.

I was just about to collapse into one of the seats at an empty table when I saw him: bright yellow hair, thick shoulders leaning over what had to be some sort of math worksheet. I hesitated, then made my way over, dropping my stuff next to him.

Riley looked up at me, then did a double-take. "Reese," he said, his voice warring between cool indifference and pure surprise. "What's up?"

"Is anyone sitting here?" I said, pointing at the rest of the empty table.

"No. All yours. Not sure how long I'm staying anyway."

I sat. It was, indeed, a math worksheet, though Riley moved as if it to hide it from my view, and I just managed not to smile.

"So," he said, flipping the paper over.

"What did you see? That night?"

"Sorry?"

I raised my gaze to his. I forgot how bright his eyes were, how much they had made me blush and stare at the ground when I had first tutored him. But that was before. Now, I had a friend to save. "The night of the party, when Charlotte disappeared. What did you see?"

"Nothing that would help us find her, if that's what you mean."

"Anything, then. Anything odd."

He frowned, folded his heavy hands over each other. "Why are you asking?"

"For obvious reasons."

He half-smiled, but it did not reach his eyes. "You mean about my text to you? Look, I'm sorry I tried to warn you off some people. It's not my business. And honestly, they had nothing to do with—at least, I'm sure they didn't—"

One thing at a time. I shook my head. Miraculously, Riley fell silent. I suppressed a sudden and maniacal urge to giggle. "I understand. It's okay. I just—I've been running over it in my head, and I know there's something I'm missing. There has to be." I paused. "You didn't come out with us, when we first went out to see Screaming Stella. The ghost," I explained, at his look of confusion. "A group of us…we went out to find the ghost, at the lakeshore. What was everyone else doing?"

He shook his head. "Sorry. I don't remember exactly. I mean, I talked to you when I brought the keg, then just caught up with some hockey guys."

"Did you see anyone at the party you didn't recognize? Someone maybe who doesn't go to our school?"

Riley's brow furrowed. "I can't think of any," he said. "Why? Do you know someone who was?"

I shrugged. I wasn't at the point yet where I was ready to share my theories of neighbors and stalkers and such— it was too early, and Riley could shoot me down or worse, tell some authority figure who would cut me off before I could go any further. "Just thought that maybe if a stranger was there, well, that's suspicious, isn't it?"

"I suppose." He drummed his fingers on the overturned worksheet, a half-eaten muffin at his left hand. Chocolate blueberry, I noted, with faint interest. Most guys I knew were obsessed with the bacon maple—something about masculinity and meat and artery clogging that all went together. "Have you asked anyone else yet? If they saw someone?"

"Not yet."

He looked pleased at this, happy to have been the first one that I came to. I blushed in turn. "Well," he said, "I'll ask around, be discrete. You never know."

"I heard Mindy," I said abruptly, "talking about how Aiden is having some sort of mental breakdown. Is that what you meant, when you said to stay away from him?"

"What? I——" Riley said, face flushing. "No, of course not. I don't—I have no idea what Mindy is talking about. Just, never mind that. I shouldn't have said anything."

"Because I don't think he is," I said, watching Riley's face carefully. A wall went up; I was sure of it, something hard and fierce that slammed shut over his eyes. "In fact, he helped me yesterday—we searched Charlotte's room."

"You *what?*"

"After the police had gone through it, of course. Anyway, we didn't find much, probably because of that. Except some microphones and such."

I had said it deliberately vaguely, so that someone not in the know could assume I meant singing or speaking microphones, could picture Charlotte in front of a stage pontificating on whatever topic she wanted and coming across brilliant, because she was Charlotte Walters.

But Riley did not assume that. He stiffened, and though I saw the poker face slide on nearly immediately, I had not missed the initial look: panic, shock, discomfort. I had hit upon something. Some secret he did not want me to know.

"Microphones," Riley repeated.

"Any idea where those are from?"

He shook his head. "What did Aiden say?"

I considered lying, making up some dramatic statement of Aiden's (*I know exactly who is responsible for this and will bring them to justice!*). Instead I said, "Not much. I didn't really know what to make of it. Any ideas?"

"No."

We stared at each other, in some sort of unspoken standoff.

Finally, Riley spoke again. "Reese," he said, voice tight, "I really, really think you need to leave this alone for now. Let the police do their work."

"The police missed it though. Don't you think I should bring it to show them?"

"You could," he said carefully, "but would it really do any good? I'm sure they came across it in their search."

"They didn't know all the places to look that I did."

"It's not a good idea to look into. Just leave it to the police, okay?"

"But why?" I felt my adrenaline rising now, like a mountain lion closing in on its prey. He was lying, hiding something from me, and I wanted to know why. I wanted to grab his shoulders and shake him, demand answers.

"You don't know what Charlotte was doing. You could find something that, that—"

"Leads me to finding her?"

"No, that's not what I meant. Look, Reese—"

"Just tell me, Riley. Whatever you know, if you just tell me then I'll be able to—"

"*It doesn't matter.* It's not relevant, okay?" He shook his head, face still beet red. "Look, I'm sorry I ever frightened you before. But you can't—you have to be careful. And going around searching rooms and asking questions, *that's not careful.*"

"Neither is—" I cut off, looking down at my ringing phone. Aiden. Riley followed my gaze, the same stony look slamming down again over his face. I sent the call to voicemail. "Anyway," I said, though my train of thought had been lost, though I could feel Riley and his secrets slipping through my fingers, "you were saying?"

"Nothing. I don't know anything, Reese."

I assessed him anew. What if, I thought, heart skipping a beat, Riley was somehow involved? I thought of the figure in the boat, rowing away. What if that had been Riley? How would he get back to shore? Or maybe he knew the person who did it. Maybe even now he was throwing false trails in front of me, stating cryptic warnings, all to keep me from circling closer to the truth. Riley suddenly felt distant and alien, and I wanted nothing more than to put as much distance between him and myself.

My phone chimed. Text message from Aiden.

I pulled the phone closer to me and read it.

They've found a body.

CHAPTER 23

$\mathscr{I}$ left Riley's table without an explanation, fairly sure I was about to be sick. I pushed my way outdoors, past the smokers playing hackeysack and passing long cigarettes back and forth, through the winding paths up to the wooded, quiet spaces around the school's stadium, where I lowered myself onto a large rock and pulled out my phone again, rereading Aiden's words.

Is it her?

No response. I leaned forward on my knees, praying, promising, doing everything in my power to try and feebly, psychically ensure that it was not Charlotte, that this investigation would not end like this. I felt so small, so powerless, so helpless. I had promised her that I would find her. But not like this. It couldn't be like this.

Again the image of divers pirouetting in the water flashed before me. Except now their hands were closing around white limbs, their feet were kicking up towards the surface, they were breaking the gray water with spluttered shouts and flurries of frenzied movement as—

No.

I shook my head. It couldn't be her. It just couldn't be. I thought of the first time that I remembered Charlotte and me going swimming in the lake, at the end of middle school. We had changed into our bathing suits and run sprinting into the cold water, screaming with delight, doing flips underwater so that the lake squirted up our noses and into our ears, and we then spent the next half hour trying to knock it out of our heads on the shore. It had been late June, the sun bright, the beach white and inviting, the forest benevolent and protective. It was—surprise, surprise —like a scene from a children's fairy tale.

Charlotte had told me stories, after, as we dried off and ate the sandwiches that her mother had prepared. Stories about the lake, about the sea creatures that swam within it, about the people who tried sailing for the far shore and never reappeared. I knew some of them: the mythology of the lake seemed to be something that sustained the St. Clair population; a favorite activity, late at night, appeared to be spinning tales of this or that mysterious thing that happened at the lake, from the miraculous cure of bunions to the meeting of a mysterious boy who might have had gills and then disappeared when one turned away. I didn't believe any of it, not really, and I was sure that the people who told those stories didn't, either.

But it was different, when Charlotte was doing the telling. The stories spun out like fully formed worlds: I had shuddered and moved my toes further from the water, lest the little orb fairies she was talking about should reach out to mark me with some unseen magic that would have me trudging back to the lake in the nighttime, removing my shoes and clothes in a trance and diving in to spend the rest of eternity doing their bidding. Charlotte was a great storyteller: lyrical voice, dramatic pauses, embellished details. More, she always seemed genuinely enchanted with the mythos of St. Clair, bringing it to life in ways that made me wish, just a little, that some of it was true.

Now I felt like all of those stories had swallowed her whole, fingers clawing and grabbing, dragging her under the water. A half-sob escaped me; I pinched my arm until I got ahold of myself. It wouldn't help, not now. I would save all that for later.

I checked my phone again. Still no response from Aiden.

I needed something, anything to do. To focus on. Whether or not they had her body—*it can't be, it won't be*—that still didn't tell us what happened to Charlotte that night.

But maybe somebody could.

And as I sat there, wind whipping through the red-gold leaves around me, nostrils burning with the scent of old tobacco and musty dirt, I thought I knew exactly who.

CHAPTER 24

This time, I wasn't going to risk getting caught by a school librarian. I pulled my coat tighter around me and headed for the closest public library in town, just a few blocks past Wolfclaw.

I had barely made it half a block, however, when my phone began to ring. My mom.

I hesitated. She never called me at school. Presumably, I was in class. I ignored it.

A few seconds later, the call screen flashed again.

"Hello?" I said sheepishly.

"Where are you?"

Lying never worked on my mother. I would often marvel when Charlotte did it to her parents, spinning easy tales about sleepovers or dinners or study sessions that never materialized. She said that it was just part of being independent, part of being a teenager, but then, she had never tried any of that stuff on *my* mom. In fact, whenever we did have to make an excuse to my mom, Charlotte relied more on charm and begging than outright lies. No, my mom was all about "trust," and "honesty," and "mutual reliability." You didn't pull that kind of stuff on her.

"Outside the school."

"Tell me the cross streets. I'm coming to pick you up."

I did. She hung up—no good-bye. Which meant she was close. Sure enough, a few minutes later my mother's old sedan came rumbling up the road, pulling to a tight, angry stop in front of me.

"I called the school," my mother said, as I climbed into the warm heat of the car. She did not look at me. Instead, she pulled back onto the road and spun the car around in a tight U. Looked like we were heading back home. "Explained that I had forgotten to call you in sick."

"Thanks."

This went unacknowledged. I leaned farther back in my seat as a light drizzle began to fall, splattering across the windshield and framing the world in bright glittering orbs. The windshield wipers whined on, screeching left and right in a rhythmic motion. For a moment it felt almost cozy, sitting there on the warm leather, inhaling the faded pine of the last air freshener my mother had hung months ago, listening to the world beating against the thin but unassailable barrier that separated us from it. *Take the long way home*, I almost said to my mother, let the silence lengthen, let the day stretch out. Because there would have to be an after, a time of facing facts and finding truths, and for the moment I wanted just to close my eyes and forget about it, become lost in some eternal present.

We pulled into the drive. I took a deep breath, pulling my bag closer. It was the beige one-armed one, clunky and uncomfortable to carry but more fashionable, at least, than the sports backpack I had worn the first two years of school. My mother had bought it for me for my sixteenth birthday. Charlotte had gotten a car—I think it had embarrassed Charlotte, honestly, especially when I saw it, which just made everything more awkward. What she didn't understand was that the purse had meant more to me, because it had been a stretch for my mother: more so than a car for the Walters. And, though I had never told Charlotte this, I derived a certain set of pride from not being the kind of kid who received a laptop for my birthday, a smart phone for Christmas, and every other kind of gizmo and gadget and fashion piece to reward some ridiculous small accomplishment that I would have done anyway. I wasn't spoiled; I wore that badge with pride. Goodness knows I was plenty else.

"I'll make hot cocoa," my mother said, still in that stiff, alien voice that I didn't want to probe too deeply. She shut off the car and flicked off the headlights, turning the afternoon from warm and glowing to gray and dull. The rain began to pour harder, and we both ran the twenty feet from the parking spot to the back door, where my mother fumbled with the key until we were finally in, gasping from the cold and shaking drops of rain from our hair and shoulders.

"Sit," she said, pointing to the couch that sat in an L-shape against the back bay window. Our favorite spot to curl up together, when I was younger, and talk about our days. It felt wrong to fold myself onto those cushions now, knowing I was about to get some sort of lecture, but I did as I was told and watched the clouds thicken outside, sending the driveway and our tiny sliver of yard into darkness. My interrogation mission would have to wait.

Morty ran over and leaned his body against my leg, delighted by our unexpected midday return. I heard the kettle wheeze and whine a few minutes later; not long after, my mother came in carrying two oversized clay mugs, our favorite, filled to the brim with powder-made hot cocoa and mounds of whipped cream. She had even sprinkled what had to be last year's Christmas candy confetti on top. I raised my eyebrows, and she offered me a small smile.

"Might as well use it up."

"I feel like you're trying to lower my guard before going for the kill."

She both laughed and winced at that. "Relax, Reese. It's serious, but not like that. I'm not—well, believe it or not, I'm not upset with you. You're not in trouble—much. It's not like you do this all the time."

"I've never done it before."

"I know." She took a deep breath, raised the cream and cocoa to her lips. "So tell me. What's going on?"

I glanced up at my mother's brown eyes, crinkled and intense. She must have taken off work to come back here, I thought—or else, swapped shifts with someone tonight. She must have been really worried. A stab of guilt went through me; I loved my mother, and I didn't want her to wonder about me, to fuss. She took care of me, and I— well, I couldn't say that I took care of her, but I did take care to give her as little trouble as possible.

"They found a body," I said. Her eyes widened. She went still, very still.

"Where?"

"The lake. There were divers."

One hand fluttered to her mouth. She let it fall, and rested her chin on it. The cocoa was held suspended in the other hand, forgotten. "My goodness," she said. And then again, "My goodness. How awful."

My stomach flipped. "You think it's her?"

Her look of pity made me faint; I felt stars burst in front of my eyes, tiny dark explosions. I set down my drink and reminded myself to breathe.

"Of course we can't know anything for sure," my mother said. "Oh, honey. I'm sorry, I'm so sorry."

The sympathy was what did it to me. If I had been at school, in front of thousands of curious or suspicious or puzzled eyes, I would have bravely faced them, tracked the student body for the one suspicious figure, the single lingering clue. But now my mother reached out to grab my shoulder, and the burden of holding up that mask was gone. I began to cry.

Even as I cried I was embarrassed, a little horrified by my own display of weakness. I managed to get it together twice before breaking down again; the third time, I finally resorted to pinching my leg until I felt a jolt of pain, which pushed back the remaining tears. Still I felt them hovering at the edge, ready to come back at one kind word. I looked at the ground and forced myself to take a sip of the now lukewarm hot cocoa.

"It's fine," I said, though of course it wasn't—it was just one of those things that you said because saying it made it seem like maybe, at one moment, it could be true.

My mother gathered up my mug and, as I dried my eyes and blew my nose, nuked my drink in the microwave, bringing it back to me with the whipped cream sagging and fizzing, disappearing into the hot cocoa below. "Want me to top that up?" she asked, and I started to refuse before nodding, because why not, after all? She went back to the fridge, retrieved the whipped cream, and sprayed another healthy dollop on top. It was, we both agreed, the best part about drinking cocoa.

"It's not going to be easy for you, these next few months," my mother said, when we had settled back in. She had tucked her legs, still in scrubs, underneath her on the saggy green cushions. "We might want to get you into therapy."

"No, Mom."

"I'm not sure I'm asking, Reese. I may be telling you."

I made myself not roll my eyes. Sure, therapy was good and blah blah blah, but I did not want to confront my own mental state right then. I wanted to focus on Charlotte. On justice. "Can we at least wait? A little bit?"

"I won't make any calls yet," she said. "Or at least, I'll just look up how to get it through insurance, okay? But no appointments. Not right now."

"Okay," I said, wishing I knew a little bit more about insurance and how likely they were to cover teenage tragedies. It's not that I had anything against therapy, per se—I knew plenty of girls that loved to brag about how often they went, as if they were just *so* complicated and special (in addition to the students who no doubt used it more quietly, for a variety of reasons)—but I wasn't ready yet to move into a world where the focus would suddenly be turned back on me: how was I feeling? What was I doing to cope? What would happen to me in the future? It felt wrong, dirty, a betrayal.

"Maybe," my mother said, hesitating. As if on cue, lightning cracked through the sky, so close that the thunder rolled right after, shaking the foundation of our townhouse. I leaned further back into the sofa. Morty shuddered and hopped up next to me, nestling into the crook of my arm as the storm raged outside. I scratched him behind his ears, leaning over to envelop him in a hug.

"Maybe," my mother tried again, "we should look at moving."

My head snapped up. "*Moving*?"

"Yes. Don't look shocked. I've thought about it a lot, since we came here. Every year, in fact."

"What?! But—but this is home." As I said it I knew it was true, even though I still told kids I wasn't from St. Clair when they asked, even though I still named one of the three other towns we had shifted between before my mother had finally moved us here. St. Clair wasn't my hometown, it would never be in my blood like it was for the other kids, but it was decidedly and irrevocably home. I felt wounded that my mother had even suggested it.

"Well, we haven't moved, have we? And for good reason. We get a great deal here, and my job is good—very good. It's not easy to just up and change your life, especially with a kid."

"Gee, sorry," I said, and my mother smirked.

"You know what I mean. Things have just been—easy enough, here. So I've thought about it, even talked with a headhunter once, but in the end I could never be sure it was much of an improvement."

"But *why?*"

"Why leave?" She gave me a curious, searching look, reading the naked confusion on my face. "You don't see it?" Then, "No, I suppose you wouldn't. You're just a kid, after all."

"I'm seventeen."

"Yes, well." She fluttered her hand, dismissing the fact. "When you've traveled a bit more, gone to college, stayed in a too-small apartment in a city, met all sorts of people— then you'll know, if you come back here." Her voice had taken on a sad, almost nostalgic quality. "St. Clair—well, it's a beautiful place. Picturesque. Safe. Good schools. And somehow, I managed to find some affordable housing in it. It's just…sometimes, it's all a little too perfect, and a little too weird all at once."

"What, like *The Stepford Wives?*" I thought about the pearl-clad mothers in their brightly patterned dresses or yoga pants showing off slim thighs, tight Botoxed faces air-kissing each other in school parking lots outside of soccer games.

"No, no. You'd find that anywhere like this. There's… something else here. Something a little rotten." Her face softened when she saw mine. "I'm sorry, darling, I know you love it here. I don't mean to speak badly of it, it's just…well." She straightened a bit, even as another clap of lightning lit the room. This time the thunder was slower, almost languid. "Do you remember your freshman year? When I had the parent-teacher conference with your math teacher?"

I did. Ms. Cayman. She was a beautiful woman, delicate features, black eyes and black curled hair, maybe twenty-five or twenty-six. Bird-like wrists and soft dresses with ballet flats; she looked like she had stepped out of some 1960s film. Her voice was soft and soothing, and even the chalk glided silently across the board when she used it. I was good at math; Ms. Cayman had seen it. She had written encouraging smileys on my tests and asked me to come up and solve the most difficult problems on the board, when we worked through them as a class.

And then we had my parent-teacher conference. Ms. Cayman was at her desk in the light dusk of the evening. It had felt wrong and even eerie being in the school at that time, like we had entered some upside-down world where the teachers taught at night, to classrooms full of invisible ghosts. I was there because Ms. Cayman had requested that I attend, and I wasn't nervous until I stepped into the room and saw Ms. Cayman's expression.

My mother stopped short as well; she knew I was a good student, and the intense worry, almost fright, on Ms. Cayman's face baffled her. She glanced down at me, then back at Ms. Cayman, and then strode forward to shake Ms. Cayman's hand. The math teacher offered it almost as an afterthought, chewing on her cheeks, gesturing us towards the two seats facing her desk.

"You're not from St. Clair, are you, Reese?" she asked me, though she was staring at my mother. The same strange fright was on her face, her skin pale, drained.

"No, not originally."

"Oh. Oh, yes, I thought so." She shuffled the papers on her desk.

We waited. My mother had a habit of letting silence linger, waiting for the other person to fill it. I think she learned that from her job, where patients were more likely to open up if you gave them the space to unspool, rather than feeding them questions and directions and seeing them on their way.

"So unusual," Ms. Cayman had said. "And yet you seem fine. They haven't gotten to you, not yet."

"What?" I said, as my mother twitched beside me.

"What are you talking about, Ms. Cayman?" my mother said, her voice firm, even. Her patient voice.

Ms. Cayman half-laughed. "Oh, don't mind me. So sorry. Silly. Reese, you're an excellent math student, you know that?" She turned her gaze towards my mother. "You moved here, too. From somewhere else."

"Obviously."

Ms. Cayman gave her a pained smile. "You're doing well? Also?"

"Ms. Cayman, I'm doing fine, and I'd like to discuss my daughter's performance in your math class. Please. Like I came here to do."

"Well, it's fine. Great, like I said." Ms. Cayman blinked her big black eyes, which suddenly seemed glassy, doll-like. The sky outside had darkened to black, and I felt the hairs on the back of my neck prick up. I was happy that my mother was with me; I felt somehow, maniacally, that if I were alone and those black eyes turned on me…

"It's so beautiful here," Ms. Cayman said. "But there's so much, so much that you can't understand." She began tapping the top of her desk, quick and rhythmic. My mother stood, pulled me up by my elbow.

"She's not usually like this," I said, as my mother gave me a light shove towards the door. I didn't care that Ms.

Cayman could hear; I was increasingly certain that whatever that was, it was not my math teacher.

"Dear God," my mother said, as I was two feet from the door. I turned back and she shooed me away, straightening quickly. But I could see Ms. Cayman rocked back in her chair, eyes rolling. And, though I didn't know how we could have missed it, not when we had sat down just two minutes before, I saw the pool of blood at Ms. Cayman's feet, a dark and inky stain on the navy carpet. "Yes," my mother said, the only sane thing now in that room. "I need an ambulance at the St. Clair High School."

We had barely spoken of that night, after. Ms. Cayman took a leave of absence—some of the nastier rumors mentioned anorexia, or something untoward with a student. I thought she must have had a nervous breakdown, or perhaps lost so much blood through some weird illness that it had affected her brain, at least temporarily. My mother would not speculate. And then three months later, paler but just the same, Ms. Cayman had reappeared, with her thin wrists and her soft, melodic voice. Just the same, but she never once called on me again, and my tests, no matter how high my scores, contained only the circled number on top, with no smileys or words of encouragement.

"What about Ms. Cayman?" I said, and then shivered, and wished, in a burst of superstitiousness, that I had not used her name.

"That poor woman. She had some mental problems, I'm sure. It's just—I've met so many women like her here, Reese."

"Mentally unstable?"

"No. Smart, attractive, for lack of a better word, *normal*, but you get another layer under, you get to know them a little more and…" She snapped her fingers and shrugged. "It's the same with the whole town. Like the parks. Beautiful, but if you try to plant anything there, it shrivels right up."

"You weren't *supposed* to plant rose bushes there anyway."

"Yes, but, the point is—well. I think, on the whole, everything and everyone is a little too cut off here. It's not good for people's nerves. Not good for the environment. What? You look as though you think I've gone off the deep end."

It wasn't that. I had heard rumors about St. Clair the entire time I'd lived there—about the lake and its monsters and mermaids, the oak tree that giggled at dusk, the old man who lived near the corner store that had garden gnomes: not the plastic or porcelain ones from a yard store, but real-life ones that walked around and snarled and bit if you got too close. Stories, they were all stories, but they were part of St. Clair's charm, all the more exciting because you knew, viscerally, they weren't true. Still, sometimes I wondered. Sometimes people seemed a little *too* keen on those stories, and I had thought that maybe they all suffered from the same mass delusion, the same desire to believe that their little town was *so* special that it was almost magic. Sometimes, I wished it was, too.

"You think it drives people to have nervous breakdowns?" I said, deliberately narrowing the scope of her statement.

"Maybe. I don't know. All I know is, I'm happy you're

going to college next year. Good for you to get out. Charlotte, too."

Lightning flashed. We both braced for the thunder, but when it came it was faint, distant. I pulled out my phone: still no answer from Aiden. An image flashed into my head: the Walters family, at some coroners' office, a blanket pulled up to Charlotte's gray-green shoulders, someone, probably Mr. Walters, saying in a broken voice "That's her," while Mrs. Walters clung to Aiden and sobbed into his shoulder. I shook my head.

"It'll be all right, darling," my mother said. "You do what you have to, but you be careful."

"How do you know what I'm doing?" I said.

She smiled. "You're my daughter. I know you. You're trying to figure out what might have happened to your friend."

I leaned my head back against the couch cushion. "Aiden practically accused me of having something to do with it, this morning."

"Ignore him. He's distraught. He'll probably apologize to you soon."

"I was almost with her, though, Mom. I followed her out, but I couldn't find her..." My throat constricted.

My mom was silent, pressing her palms into the side of her mug again as she let her head drop forward. "It's not your fault, Reese. Whatever happens. Remember that."

Ice shot through me. *Whatever happens.*

"Can I take the car?" I said, setting down my mug and standing up. "I need to go talk to someone. At the school."

My mother checked her watch. "I need to do a few things first. I'll be back by two or three. Will that work?"

I could have asked her to drop me off, but there was a football game that day. Which meant that, at four o'clock, I'd know exactly where to find who I was looking for.

Danny.

"That's fine," I said. I wanted to get this right, because I'd only have one chance to surprise him. I'd work on it that afternoon. "Three by the latest?"

"Yes." She kissed my forehead, like she used to do when I was a little girl. And then she left, and I was alone with Morty and with my silent, mournful phone, waiting for the text that would tell me that my worst nightmare had come true, that Charlotte was truly, irrevocably gone.

CHAPTER 25

*B*y the time I arrived, the game was in its final quarter. The thunder had stopped, but a light drizzle turned everything gray and blurry, and I pulled my jacket tighter around me, taking care not to slip on the wet leaves as I made the long walk from the parking lot to the stadium.

The crowd was thin for one of the St. Clair games—we were actually pretty good, and followed avidly by the approximately two million family members and friends of the way-too-many guys on the football team, which did not enforce cuts except by punishing physical fitness and psychological intimidation, and which resorted only to benching those players, for seasons and years, who were not good enough.

But the rain, and the fact that the game was on a Tuesday, and not to a rival, had cut the crowd down to something manageable. Miserable cheerleaders in thick rain coats were milling about the sidelines, apparently taking a break or deciding that the 35-3 scoreline meant that they had done their job for the night. I could smell cigarette smoke mixed with the acridness of turf as I turned into the stadium.

My mother's words haunted me as I made my way towards the bleachers, aware of eyes turning towards me, sure I could hear the rise of whispers as I found a seat near the bottom and sat down, after an ineffectual wipe of the rain collected on the metal surface. I glanced around the stadium, at the glowing scoreboard, at the collection of white and blue spandexed bodies on the turf, holding helmets or blinking up at the rain. The game had slowed to a snail's pace; there was not much left to fight for. I searched the faces of the blue players, especially: they were not from St. Clair. Could they tell that the town was different somehow? Mystical in a way that I didn't fully understand?

Even as the rain fell and the clouds darkened the sky, I felt strange and disconnected. For a moment I felt like I was falling to the back of the telescope, seeing the scene all through some distant lens. I could hear the click of the coach's pen on his clipboard, could feel the shivers of the parents near the gate, clutching coffee cups in between whitened fingers. The raindrops became individual crystals, glittering and lethal. The wind that howled behind me, snaking down through the bleachers and onto the field, seemed to carry a message with it, whispers of my name. *Look back, look back.*

I turned. Mindy Tilden was marching towards me.

It was at the same moment that the world tilted again, and I noticed something that I hadn't when first walking into the stadium: everything, everyone, was oriented towards Charlotte.

It was in the way all eyes were turned towards me, fingers pointing and lips whispering. The number of newspapers clutched in their hands, with that small and unhelpful article updating the town on Charlotte's disappearance. But if the press was not talking, the people certainly were: I saw, with something like fear, the "Find Charlotte" buttons that were pinned on a few chests. Who had made those? Who had even had time, in two days?

Mindy was flanked by two other field hockey girls, Luisa and Greta or Lucinda and Gigi, I could never remember. Charlotte kept her field hockey friendships mostly separate from the rest of her life; she was not part of the "main clique," she would tell me, using scare quotes with her fingers, and as such the only times Mindy and Charlotte ever hung out were mandatory team dinners or social events, when the girls would make snide comments or thinly veiled digs and erupt into peals of vicious laughter.

"Hey," Mindy said, an aggressive challenge. "What are you doing here?"

I lifted an eyebrow. "It's a football game."

Mindy shared a scathing look with Luisa/Lucinda. "I've never seen you come to them before. Especially alone."

I didn't know you followed my movements so closely, I almost said. But I didn't need this, not now, not with so many people watching. "What do you want, Mindy?"

She crossed her arms. Her face was at once defensive, embarrassed, accusatory. She hesitated, then slipped onto the seat next to me. Her friends took protective positions one bleacher up, leaning forward so they could hear.

"I came to warn you," she said. "About Aiden."

My memory flashed back to the library, where Mindy had mentioned they used to date. I didn't like this, somehow, for reasons I didn't really care to explore. I braced myself for the worst.

"He's hiding things," Mindy said. "I mean, he's not a bad guy, but you should be careful with him. I saw you in his car the other day."

"Okay." I wasn't going to give her anything, wasn't going to try to explain that *my* best friend was missing and *his* sister was missing, so it was only natural that the two of us were going to talk about it.

She waited, searching my face. "I don't know what he's told you," she said, "but he's…he's a really good liar."

"What do you mean?"

Mindy shook her head. "It's private. I don't want to get into it. You know that we dated earlier this year?"

I tried, and probably failed, to feign mild surprise. "No, I didn't."

"Yeah, well. Most people didn't. I wanted to keep it kind of private." Or he did, I thought nastily, and then felt a stab of guilt. If he *had*, I thought, it was a knock against him: no one but a jerk would suggest keeping a romance under wraps. "He has issues. I'm not going to say what I'm talking about, out of respect for him, but—well, you should know."

"Okay," I said again. "Well—thanks. But I'm not really focused on Aiden right now."

I turned my shoulder to her, but Mindy did not get up and leave. "Any news about Charlotte?" she asked.

"No." *They found a body in the lake.*

"Just be careful," Mindy said. "I'm not saying he had anything to do with it—"

"Maybe you should talk to the police," I cut in. "If you have some information. And if you don't want to tell me specifics."

Her face slammed closed. "What, you think I'm lying?"

"No. But I'm not sure what I'm supposed to do with 'be careful.'"

Mindy snorted. "Just trying to be a *friend*," she said, standing up and dusting off her legs. She gave me a look like I was gum on the bottom of her shoe. "Jeez. You know I found something in his room that night? But you wouldn't believe me about that, either."

"What were you doing in his room?"

"Wouldn't you like to know." Her friends stood as well, giving me unreadable stares. I felt the heat from a dozen other gazes watching the scene unfold and blushed.

"Well, what did you find in his room?"

"I don't have to tell you anything. I'm trying to *help* you. Take it or leave it."

We stared at each other, Mindy with real venom in her eyes. If this were some teen movie, she would be the nemesis, the beautiful, popular girl with an axe to grind against the Walters family because she couldn't ever aspire to be even a tenth of what they were. She would be mean with nothing else underneath, cruel with no depth. But she wasn't. I remembered Mindy in middle school, helping me pick up the one hundred pens that scattered across the hallway during passing time, even as a few boys hooted and hollered and shouted "free pens!" as they crushed them underneath their feet. Mindy chatting with me in line for muffins in the morning, asking me for help on some math assignment, complimenting me just because she was always ready to do that, always willing to highlight something in someone else that she admired. I had seen her do it in typing class once, when a shy girl was being mocked by some juniors ahead of us. Mindy had turned around, loudly complimented her, and then asked if they could be partners on an upcoming assignment. The relief was so palpable on the girl's face that I almost heard it.

Certainly high school had changed all of us since then. Junior year had been taut, competitive. Mindy had, like everyone else, disappeared for weeks to study and grind, and reappeared at parties with a little too much gusto—not drinking, because she didn't drink, at least not really—but with a brightness burning in her eyes that spoke of worries she was trying to avoid, burdens that she was desperately trying to escape. I had wondered sometimes, perhaps not often enough, if there was something else behind that, something beyond just the frantic energy we all had to finish applications, to score well, to prove that we could become something. I had never been close enough to ask.

"Thanks," I said, and I tried to alter my voice, enough that it sounded sincere. "I appreciate it, but I don't need any warning. I just want to find Charlotte."

They found a body.

Mindy blinked. She looked like she couldn't quite decide how she wanted to act, if she wanted to take my words as mocking, or if she wanted to somehow continue the battle that she had obviously come here to start. "Well," she said. "That's fine. I do too." She drew in a breath. "Just—you'll remember what I said?"

"Yes."

When she had gone, something strange and inscrutable in her expression, I turned back towards the game and warmed my hands with my breath. A few minutes left, now. The movements of the athletes were languid, almost bored. A kick down the field veered sharply sideways, and the players shuffled forward at something that could hardly be called a jog.

My mind kept skipping back to Mindy, to the expression that was on her face. I didn't know what was going on in her life, and I couldn't, but my mother's words came back to haunt me now, and the memory of something else, something Charlotte had told me early on when we had first become friends.

I had been so gloriously happy, back in those days, thrilled that I had somehow been chosen, knowing that I was unworthy of the honor. I had been so cringingly eager to please, so willing to subsume my will to hers. I must have been maddening.

There was just one area, though, where I perhaps was different. Whenever Charlotte and I talked about anything, we managed a back-and-forth that felt easy, natural, enlivening. We disagreed more often than not, about all the big philosophical things and none of the details, which made it easy to slip into long discussions where we were on staunchly opposite sides, but where none of it seemed to matter, not to us at the moment, anyway. And while I was ready to do any activity that Charlotte suggested, and was ready to take her opinion on any person at school as gospel, here I was decidedly myself. I had a will of my own. Sometimes, I wonder if that's what saved the friendship for her—if I had just blindly agreed to her viewpoints, tried to suss out her thoughts and then mimic them exactly, if she would have dropped me like she had so many other girls. I had never gotten up the courage to ask.

One day, near the end of eighth grade, we had gone out to the tennis courts after school and climbed the wall behind them, a small, steep set of rocks that, it was rumored, at least a dozen kids had broken their arms climbing (which made it a special challenge that every student felt compelled to undertake before graduation). We pulled ourselves onto little outcrops of rock, hands roughened by the stone, jeans scratched up with dirt and muck.

"Do you think all of this is real?" Charlotte had asked, sweeping her hand out towards the school and the grounds. "Or just a mirage? Like some video game."

"What?" I said, smiling. "Like our bodies are plugged in somewhere and this is all just virtual reality?"

"I guess. Or…like a dream. A big dream."

I considered, really considered. A breeze drew the scent of wet moss towards me; leaves and branches rustled. I closed my eyes and thought, *if any place is a dream, it must be this one*, because St. Clair was at once more beautiful and more mysterious than any place I had ever been.

But I didn't say this to Charlotte, because she was from St. Clair, because she wouldn't understand, not fully and not ever, the wonder with which I viewed the town. So instead I said, "I guess it's possible. But then how do you ever tell that you're really real? That this is reality and not…" I flicked my hand, indicating all the rest. Dream. Mirage. Video game.

Charlotte grinned. "I guess you only need to if it would change anything."

"What do you mean? It would change everything."

"Would it?" Charlotte swiveled towards me, eyes bright. "If this were a video game, and you were trapped, and nothing you were ever going to do would change that, what would you do differently?"

"I don't know. Take everything a little less seriously."

"But pain would be the same. Loss. Pleasure."

"Yes, but it wouldn't be *real*."

"What does that matter? It would be real to you."

"No," I said, "because I would know it was an illusion."

I geared myself up for an argument, a battle of ideas, something I relished just as much in those days as Charlotte. But instead of shooting something back, she considered me for a long time. I blushed under the scrutiny, wondering if I had missed something, not sure why Charlotte had gone from playful to serious in the span of only a few seconds.

"That means you're realer than everyone else here," she said. "You know what I would do? I'd keep on doing the exact same thing."

I laughed, but mostly to hide my confusion. I didn't know what Charlotte was playing at.

"Everyone else would, too," she said, leaning her head back and closing her eyes. I stiffened; it couldn't have been easy to balance like that, to prevent your stomach from lurching, your limbs from twisting off the precarious perch… "Sometimes I feel like St. Clair isn't real, you know? Only things outside of it are. Like you and your mom."

"What do you mean? Of course it's real."

She peeked one eye open. "Not in the same way. St. Clair could float off from the rest of the world and it would keep on ticking just like it always has. Nothing would change."

"Oh," I said, relaxing as I thought I understood. "You mean that it's independent."

"Absolutely. Don't you think so? It's why when people like you come in, everything gets a little ruffled. St. Clair isn't used to outsiders."

I thought she was talking like some of the other kids did, in spooky hyperbole when they tried to scare me, when they took what I thought was unnecessary and almost aggressive pride in the fact that most people had grown up here, and most people, after a few youthful travels, never left. I had grown a little silent then, a little sullen, because I hadn't expected Charlotte of all people to try to scare me about it.

"It's a good thing," she said, reading my expression. "You're better than the rest of us. You aren't—your blood isn't—"

"The same as yours?"

"No, better. You're the only real girl here. The last real girl." She smiled at me, but I couldn't follow her logic, couldn't understand why she was searching me so intently now, looking for a response that I couldn't give. "Anyway," she said, shrinking back, disappointed. "You'll see. Never mind."

We had parted in the closest thing to a fight that we had had since meeting, me feeling uneasy, unsettled, and even slighted, Charlotte frustrated and feeling misunderstood. We clawed our way tentatively back to a truce in the next few days, trading polite, cold greetings, then asking utilitarian questions about homework and classes, and then finally cracking the odd joke here and there that broke the ice and renewed our warmth towards each other. We did not talk about St. Clair again, not in that way. I had always assumed that some older kid had put ideas into Charlotte's head; I didn't know what she thought of me. The truth was, I loved St. Clair. I wanted to belong to it. I did not like being called out as separate, as being other.

And now? The final buzzer on the game went off, and the football players shuffled from the field. To me, Charlotte Walters had been the realest thing about this town. And now that she was gone, everything seemed a dangerous illusion, a rotten mirage.

I stood up. My eyes searched the crowd, landing finally on the spandex-clad Danny Evans. As if summoned, his gaze flicked up to meet mine.

Go time.

CHAPTER 26

*I*t surprised me, how easy it was to convince Danny to meet me at the coffee shop after the game. He floated to the chain link fence, acceded to my suggestion with a quick nod of his head and a request to give him thirty minutes to change. I thought about the possibility that he was dodging me and decided to wait outside the locker rooms for him so that we could walk over to Wolfclaw together.

Danny Evans had always been one of those boys who floated in Charlotte's orbit without ever gaining her attention—at least, until recently. He was a second-string football player and mediocre lacrosse player, dabbled in debate team and volunteered to bolster his college application, and spent most of the rest of his time chasing girls and doing his best to appear not to care, about anything and everything. I never remembered him drinking or smoking much at parties, but I could always remember his laugh, harsh and high, usually at the expense of whoever was that night's target. Not an instigator—I thought I would remember that—but someone willing to sacrifice someone else on the altar to bolster his own reputation.

The only true memory I had of him, when I could distinguish his face from the dozen other athletes that floated in and out, was sophomore year, when we had been on a field trip to a nearby nature preserve. The trip had involved a hike through a tick-infested forest; three students had to have the bloodsuckers removed with tweezers by grim-faced teachers, and so it became a favorite trick of a group of football players to tickle the back of people's necks with grass or leaves or anything else that would send that creeping sensation shooting from your head to your feet.

They didn't try it on Charlotte—they didn't dare—but one or two came up to try and do it to me as a proxy.

"You touch her, you die," Charlotte said, swiveling around to the first. He grinned sheepishly and peeled off.

We came finally to a wide field dotted with picnic tables, where we were ostensibly supposed to sit and have lunch. The teachers had a brief, strained conversation about the long grass while the rest of us were instructed to stay near the trail, on the other side of which was a long, shallow river gurgling over gray and pink stones.

Most of us were alternating between standing on the dirt trail and balancing on some of the larger stones that lined the river. The drop was only a few feet, and the stones that lined it were wide and flat, easy to keep your balance as long as you didn't try anything stupid. That didn't, of course, stop a number of boys from accepting that challenge. They jumped from stone to stone, dared each other to balance on one foot and touch their toes, stole phones from one another and tossed them, high and arching, above the heads of other students. One clattered a foot down the way, skidding to a stop against an exposed root. The boy in question swore and leaned forward to retrieve it, cursing his friends even as they grinned and hooted around him.

"Idiots," Charlotte breathed. We were sharing space on one of the large stones next to the river. I turned to watch the teachers gesticulate at the path and then back at the tables. One of them, Mrs. Perez, began to shake her head vehemently and make firm cutting motions with her hands.

Charlotte stiffened. I turned to follow her gaze.

Some of the football boys were creeping up behind a girl in our class, Sarah Rice, who was quiet and pudgy and small as a mouse, and jumpy as one too. She had been walking alone, as she usually did, and was now stopped on one of the large stones like the rest of the students, back turned towards the rest of the scene. She seemed caught up in the flow of the river, contemplating it with her small hands folded behind her back, dressed in a pressed white cardigan and a skirt that was just a few inches too long to look modern.

"Hey!" Charlotte shouted, but it was too late.

Danny reached down and gave the stone Sarah was standing on a quick, ferocious wiggle. They laughed as her hands began to pinwheel and her legs danced maniacally as she sought some hold. To be fair, I don't think they meant what happened next, but they should have expected it.

Sarah was not able to regain her balance. The boys sunk back, bursting with suppressed laughter, as Sarah tipped, tipped, and finally fell over. Her body hit like a sack of rocks, the thuds jaw-clenching as she smacked once, twice, and finally fell into the stream. Heads swiveled; bodies tensed. Kids leaned forward with breaths held, trying to see if she was still moving. Somewhere behind us, one of the teachers swiveled and rushed over.

Sarah's body was caked in mud, a great splotch of it across her middle and down one leg, her neatly tied bun completely askew. For a moment she lay still at the bottom of the stream, stunned. And then she raised herself onto all fours, limbs shaking, and in the two inches of water shouted, in a great panic, "I'm drowning!"

A teacher jumped over the stones and slid down to her, helping Sarah pick up her ruined book bag, her water-logged phone. Sarah turned beet red as she realized that she was not, in fact, about to die, and looked like she was fighting hard to keep back tears. Sometimes, when I look back to that day, I thought it would have been better if she had cried. At least then the collective sympathy would have been roused for her, for it was a nasty trick. But that dramatic statement was what did it: the giggles tittered through the crowd of students, low and venomous, and Danny and his friends were doubled over in painful laughter, eyes watering.

Charlotte's eyes blazed. "Come on," she said to me, and we spent the next two hours of the field trip (the picnic tables were abandoned, and we ended up lunching on the side of the trail) following the football boys a little too closely. Charlotte managed to steal three of their phones—not Danny's—and dumped them into a stream, behind a tree, and down a port-a-potty, but she grew irritable and then incensed when the trip ended and she had still not extracted Danny's.

I had made noises about how it wasn't worth it, about how we perhaps should try to talk to Sarah instead. But I didn't try very hard; Sarah looked wet and miserable and withdrawn, inside the long coat of one of the teachers, and I felt that any attempt to make conversation with her would draw too much attention, would make it obvious that we pitied her, and would lead only to scorn.

"It's fine," Charlotte had spat finally, as we walked up the long drive to the school, and it was clear her game was up. The boys had caught on now to the fact that they were losing phones left and right; most of them were guarding them jealously in their hands, though no one had yet put together that the missing phones were not the result of hiking, but Charlotte's nimble fingers. "I'll get him back another time."

I tried to remember if she ever had.

Danny and I made it to Wolfclaw Coffee a little after five; Danny offered to drive us, but it was only a couple of blocks, and I preferred to walk. His hair was still wet from his post-game shower, and he seemed different somehow, as if in the space of just three days he had grown older, shadows multiplying across his face.

The coffee shop was filled with a few parents and younger kids who had most likely been at the football game, too, fingers curled around warm coffee cups as they laughed and chatted and made noises about how they would *have* to get together soon, everything had just been so crazy…

Danny slunk into a seat near the door. "Do you want

anything?" I asked, scanning the chalkboard menu. I found myself suddenly nervous, and a strangely and deliciously flavored latte would certainly help.

"Uh, hot chocolate," Danny said.

I almost told him to get up and order it himself, perhaps a little more nicely. But he was there at my request, and I wanted him to be comfortable, to feel like he could tell me anything. "Right up," I said, possibly too chirpy. To my surprise, though, Danny, shaking himself awake, fumbled in his wallet and handed me a ten.

I ordered our drinks separately, paying for my Earl grey latte with my own crumpled five. The barista smirked at me as I paid twice, separately, probably thinking this was some adolescent date gone wrong. I blushed.

The sounds of steaming milk and clunking machinery drowned out the rest of the shop for a moment. I floated over to the community signs, running my gaze over notices about neighborhood block parties, upcoming plays at the theater, and marches for causes associated with pink or blue or yellow ribbons. My eyes froze at a sheet stuck near the bottom, a picture of Charlotte, her school yearbook picture, with only the text, *Have you seen this girl?* A phone number was underneath. I googled it while waiting for the drinks. The police department.

I shivered.

With Charlotte's poster eyes watching me, I took the two drinks as my name was called and hurried back to the table near the window where Danny was hunched over. He glanced up at me, searching my face as I slid across from him, jerking when our pinkies accidentally touched. I dumped the change in front of him, and he pocketed it in silence.

"Thanks for meeting me," I said.

"Yeah, sure." He leaned back in his chair, eyes scanning the room, probably looking for anyone who would recognize the two of us sitting together. It *would* look suspicious, I thought: I rarely hung out with any of the athletes on my own, really with *any* boys on my own, and with Charlotte missing…but I couldn't worry about that right now.

"Listen, about that night—" I began.

"I need you to help me," Danny said, at the same time. He broke off, reddening. My mouth snapped shut.

"With what?" I said, mostly to fill the silence that had spread like poison between us and threatened to cut off the meeting in a cloud of awkwardness.

Danny shook his head and looked left, out at the darkening afternoon. The sun was sunk low in the sky, illuminating the slate gray into the faintest tendrils of pink and orange, harbingers of the sunset. His face looked different in the light, stripped and vulnerable.

"Nothing," he said, not looking at me. "Just—you go first. What about that night?"

"I was wondering if you saw anything. Heard anything, right before—"

"Why would you think that?" Danny said sharply. I flinched, and he sucked in his breath. "Sorry. I just mean—my nerves are fried. Obviously because we'd been kind of hanging out, the police are asking me stuff."

I went still and tried very, very hard to contain my shock. *Hanging out?* Did he mistake Charlotte being kind to him for a few hours as some kind of larger interest? Or was there something else about Charlotte that I didn't know?

Regardless, I was her best friend. He wouldn't expect me to be in the dark. "Yeah, how long ago did that start?" I asked again. "She was a little secretive about it at first— just said some guy on the football team until, I don't know, a week or so ago." My heart quickened; the detail could have been wildly off, but I needed something to bluff with, to make him think that I knew more than I did.

Danny cast me a suspicious look. "A few weeks. A little more, maybe. Nothing serious. Just hanging out some."

"Of course."

"We weren't dating."

"I know you weren't."

He nodded vehemently. "You'll tell the police that, then? If they come and ask you? They've been out to visit twice now, trying to make it seem like I was jealous of Charlotte, like she was two-timing me."

"Well, she couldn't have been, if you weren't dating."

"Huh? Oh, yeah. Yeah, that's right! But she wasn't h— she wasn't dating anybody." He cast another quick glance up at me for confirmation and straightened when I nodded, giving it to him. "Yeah. Stupid cops. Circling like they think *I* know something."

"Well, of course not," I said. It was a fine line: playing his side without making him realize it. Making him think I naturally just believed him, the way I'm sure his parents and teachers and friends all did. Taking his word for things because Danny was *used* to having people do that. "That's ridiculous. But I'm wondering, did you see anyone unusual at the party that night? Like, that you didn't recognize?"

He had relaxed. He had come here, I realized, to get me to believe him, to help plead his case to the cops, and in just a few sentences he thought it had been accomplished. Now he was all onboard for exploring alternate theories.

"I don't...think so," he said. "But, you know, I could be wrong. I didn't see everyone that night. Why, did you see someone?"

I shook my head. "No. I mean, when we went outside, it was six of us—you, Karuna, Eliot, Aiden, me, Charlotte." I ticked them all off on my hands. "Then we got spooked and came back in."

"You got spooked," Danny reminded me. "I would've been fine. But yeah, probably smart. Water and alcohol don't mix anyway." It sounded like a line he had been fed by his parents, for good reason.

"And then when Charlotte went back out," I said carefully, "did you see anything then?"

He fiddled with his hot chocolate cup. His foot was twitching beneath the wooden table, and I thought I could see his jaw working beneath his cheek. "I didn't see anything," he said finally. "Weren't you there?"

"You saw me leave, then?" I said. And when he opened his mouth, about to protest that he was watching us, I added, "Did you see anyone follow us?"

He thought about that, shook his head. "Though I wouldn't have put it past the brother."

"Charlotte's brother?"

He nodded again.

"Why?"

Danny shrugged. "Overprotective. He followed us out, didn't he? And he was watching, the whole night."

An image of Aiden flashed into my mind: pale like a specter, like some elven king in the night come to lead us back to safety.

"And you didn't see anyone else leave?" I pressed.

"Well, maybe," Danny said, uncomfortable. "Like you said, there were a lot of people there. Maybe someone slipped out, but…" He shrugged. "I was drinking. I don't remember. You're the one that followed her."

There was a question there, a hunger that I didn't want to address. If I had seen anything, anything at all, I would have told the police, I would have rushed down every lead. Instead I was sitting here across from the boy who apparently had had *something* going on with Charlotte (*why wouldn't she tell me?*), who was frightened of the police and who was more interested in making sure I didn't get him into trouble than in helping me find Charlotte.

"You know about the prank she was going to pull, though, don't you?" Danny said.

This time, my blank face gave me away too quickly.

"You don't?" he said, flabbergasted, pushing his hot chocolate away from him. "Seriously? But you guys are, like, best friends."

I know, like, obviously, I felt like shooting back, but held my tongue. "What prank are you talking about?"

He shook his head in amazement. "Were you guys fighting or something? Because if so, you probably need to go to the police." I could see the wheels turning in his head. Or *he* could go tell the police, try to get himself out of their spotlight by knocking it onto me.

"We weren't fighting," I said tightly. "Maybe she was

going to surprise me, too. What prank are you talking about?"

"With the dead girl."

"What?"

He shook his head. "You know, the ghost girl. Screaming Stella. When we all went out there, and Aiden showed up. She was going to disappear for a minute, and then Screaming Stella was going to come out in all white... you didn't know about this?"

Apparently it took him hearing the answer a hundred times for it to register. "No, I didn't. So what happened?"

"Well Aiden came, obviously. And then you freaked out. I thought you knew about it, and knew that she couldn't do it anymore, with Aiden there. So you got us all back by pretending to be sick."

I hadn't been sick. I had been scared, scared of the night and the forest and the sudden nefarious and mystical mood that had descended upon us, as if we had crossed the threshold into some forbidden kingdom.

"Okay. So...you think that's what she was doing afterwards? Going to try and do the prank again?"

"What? No." Danny's face screwed up. "No one was out there. Who would she be pranking?"

"Well, I followed her." As she knew I would.

"Oh. Right. Well..." He frowned again. "I don't know. I guess, maybe? Do you think we—you—should tell the police that?"

"Did you already tell them about the prank?"

"Sure, yeah."

"'Sure' or 'yes'?"

"Jeez," Danny said, giving me a strange look. "*Yes,*

183

Officer Reese. I thought you were supposed to be the sweet one."

I smiled, but it was harsh and sour. "Is that what Charlotte said?"

"No." A snort. "Just smart. Crazy smart." He gave me that look again, half-fearful, half something else. "So you'll tell the police, if they ask you? We weren't dating. Nothing was going on. I wasn't even out there when—you know."

"You were at the party?"

"Yeah, I just said that."

"Did you see anything else? Anything at all. Something suspicious—did you see where Aiden went?"

Danny held up his hands. "Drunk, remember? No. I didn't. I don't even really remember the order of things that well."

The door to the café opened, and a crisp breeze whooshed around my ankles, making my hair stand on end. The stench of cigarette smoke, acrid and bitter, followed in from two of the smokers standing outside—baristas, on break.

"Anything could be helpful," I pressed. "Did anyone else know that Charlotte was planning a prank?"

"Well, I thought you did."

"Anyone else?"

"*No.*" He began to fidget, as if he were ready to leap up and leave. Indeed, I think he might have, but his eyes caught on something behind me, and I turned to follow them.

Riley.

Riley walked towards us, eyes swiveling between me

184

and Danny. "Reese," he said, pulling up a chair without being asked. "I need to talk to you."

"I'll let you guys—" Danny said, relief visible. But the door to the café opened again, and this time, we all turned to look at the newcomers.

The cops.

Officer Bordeaux and Officer Stone. They seemed not to notice us, just stood inside and leaned casually up against the glass, chatting about some code something or other, arms crossed, heads tilted back. I shuddered. I had never seen police officers before at Wolfclaw Coffee.

Danny seemed to be thinking the same thing, for he shriveled in his seat again, mumbled something about finishing his hot chocolate.

"Come walk with me?" Riley said, ignoring Danny. "It's important."

"No thanks."

"*Reese.*"

I glanced back up, startled at the urgency in his tone. The door to the café swung open again. I heard Danny curse behind me.

It was like a morbid reunion of the night of the party. For there, standing in the door to the café, eyes swinging wildly about, hooded black coat pulled tightly around him, was Aiden.

They found a body.

I stood, my heart thundering in my chest. *Was it her?* I wanted to shout. *Just tell me if it was her.*

CHAPTER 27

*I*t was just a few weeks ago that Charlotte and I had gone to the library together, not to do any schoolwork, but to climb to the top of its winding stairs to what people called the tower perch, a circular room with seat cushions and bean chairs where you could look at a 360-degree view of the town, roads snaking through buildings and trees, everything a glow of red and orange and yellow in the deepening fall.

Surprisingly, the perch was empty. Charlotte and I both pressed up against the window, watching people and cars move like little bugs beneath us. From the eastern-facing window you could see the little mirror-glint of water, while from the western-facing one you could make out the tall buildings and jagged edges of the city skyline. It was cozy up there; I always felt like I was nestled in a little cut of idyllic paradise, in between the industrial buildings and factories and barred storefronts that surrounded St. Clair, casualties of the last recession that had not yet recovered.

But the town itself was an oasis, a fortress, and when you looked out that window you could see, really see, that there was something magical and different about the place I now called home.

I could tell that Charlotte was a little off; she had been in a strange mood, these past few weeks, which I put down to the general stress of college applications and tests and everybody reminding us that we'd better enjoy this year, because soon enough it would be over and the rest of our lives would begin and then the great vortex of sad adulthood would overtake us. I mostly let her alone, when she was like this: when Charlotte wanted to talk about something, she was never shy about bringing it up.

Instead I moved to the northern-facing part of the perch, leaning up against the cushioned bench and taking in the long finger of coastline that extended up, up, up. Sometimes Charlotte and I drove along the road that ran parallel to the water, out where the big mansions were, and I would dream about what it would be like to live in one of those.

Charlotte didn't need to dream, of course—she already did.

"My grandfather died this summer, too," Charlotte said. "My mom's dad." I almost jumped; in my trance-like state, I had forgotten she was there.

"Oh!" I said. "I'm sorry." And then, when I had a moment to process it further, "You didn't tell me."

"Remember when we were all on vacation to California? Yeah, that was it."

I spun to face her, wounded and struggling not to be.

Charlotte had told me near the end of summer that instead of field hockey preseason and our final trips and sleepovers before senior year, she would be leaving for California for a small vacation. "Family thing," she had said then, rolling her eyes, and I had tried to understand because of course she wasn't ditching me; her parents probably just wanted one more good family vacation together before their son went off to college and their daughter started the final year of living at home. Charlotte had sent me pictures of towering, red-tinted sequoias, of little mountainous downtowns with general store signs slung like bumper plates across rickety wooden front doors, white linen restaurants with twisted candelabras. She had never mentioned a dying grandfather, or a funeral—only her grandmother, her father's mother, who had passed away in late June. From what I knew, Charlotte's maternal grandfather was much younger: in his late fifties or early sixties.

"Your grandfather?" I said. "You never told me."

Charlotte smiled, pained and guilty. "Yeah, well. It was a lot, and also my family was being so weird about it. All secretive—like death was contagious." She paused. "Maybe it is."

"I'm sorry," I said. "Was it…I mean how did he…?"

"Cancer. It had spread." She shrugged, though her face looked yellow as she stared out the window at the town beyond, her mind drifting elsewhere, probably to a hospital room, to nurses moving and poking and prodding and smiling, to doctors rushing in and gesticulating and rushing out again, to machines that beeped and whined and signaled alerts that sent your heart racing, even though the nurses would walk briskly in and unclip something and say, "There! Much better now, hmm?"

I shook myself. "I'm sorry," I said. "When my uncle—well. I'm sorry." I felt awkward suddenly, too big for the room. Death had taken up all the space.

"I know. I'm sorry about your uncle. My grandfather—he was sixty-three, you know."

"Young," I said, because I knew I was meant to.

"Your uncle, too." She looked sideways at me. "How old was he?"

"Sixty-five. Pancreatic."

"Does that run in your family?"

"No. At least, I don't think so." I shrugged. "He was a smoker." The information that usually caused people to nod sympathetically and relax, just a fraction. *Smoker. There was a reason. It won't happen to me.*

But Charlotte did not. She looked, if anything, a little disappointed, but then the light in the perch shifted and she glanced away. "I'm sorry. My grandfather wasn't a smoker, and he died anyway. So." She shrugged. "Evidence that it doesn't matter?" But her tone was too light, the topic too dark, for the joke to ring true.

"I wish I would have known," I said, because I was too much of a coward to say what I really meant: *you should have told me.* "I would have sent flowers, or—I don't know. Something."

Charlotte laughed. "We had so many flowers. Too many. Thank goodness you didn't." She knelt on one of the benches and folded her arms on the windowsill, leaning forward to stare down, down, down. "Anyway, cycle of life, right?"

"Well, I suppose. It still sucks."

"What would you do? If you had, like, a year to live."

I blinked. It was something I had actually thought about often, since Uncle Richard died. "Probably quit school. Go travel or something. Eat just dessert, all the time."

Charlotte's lips curled into a smile. "What about if you had two years?"

"Two? I mean, probably the same."

"Right. What about five?"

I searched her expression, trying to understand what game she was playing. "Well…" I said slowly. "I don't know. Would I be healthy for those five years?"

"Let's say healthy enough."

"Okay. Well—I don't know. I'd probably try to do the same things, but maybe I'd try to accomplish something, too. Like get my college degree." No, that was a stupid idea, making my mother pay for four years of school that I'd never see a return on investment for. "Or start a business, or something. Make something that lasts longer than me."

She nodded, eyes lighting up as she twisted her neck to look at me. "Makes sense. Like a legacy."

"Yeah, I guess so."

"What about ten years?"

"You have to play, too!"

Charlotte smiled. "I will, I promise. But you first…ten years?"

I calculated. Twenty-seven. "The same stuff, probably. And same for fifteen, before you ask me."

"Twenty, then. You'd be thirty-seven."

I considered, biting off my first instinct to tell her it would be same, it would all be the same: enjoy things, try to make something lasting. But then...thirty-seven. That was middle-age, wasn't it? Though my mother had laughed once when I said her thirty-eight-year-old coworker was middle-aged. I had always pictured by that time, I'd have a family, a husband and two or three kids and a dog like Morty at my heels. It would be the middle of my life, in some ways the height of it, everything slowing down and speeding up all at once.

"Well," I said. "I don't know. I guess it wouldn't be fair to start a family."

"What if you had thirty? If you were forty-seven?"

"Then maybe? I don't know—why are you asking?"

Charlotte held my gaze for a few beats, searching. Then she laughed, shrugging, and fell back into her seat. "Never mind. Just wondering. You probably remember, with your uncle. Lots of morbid thoughts, thinking about wasting time, blah blah blah."

She had told me, then, of the funeral, of the dozens and dozens of family members and cousins and great-aunts and great-uncles who had descended on the California funeral home, faces yellow and somber, the only buoyancy in the little kids that ducked in and out of parental legs in their little tuxes and fluffed dresses, so young that they only saw a reunion and not a tragedy. She told me of the family fights that escalated into harsh whispers, and then shouts, at the wake, and of the sharp needling about past transgressions and old secrets that the family reunions inevitably brought out. She told me of the way that her grandfather had looked in his casket, himself but also not, stiff and a little too brightly colored, and how she had felt nauseous every time one of his old friends or her older relatives would reach down into the casket to pat him, or worse, bend down to bestow a kiss on his cold forehead.

"So I decided. I'm going to be cremated," Charlotte said, and I could tell that she was aiming for her tone to be light, but there was something darker there, something more unpleasant.

"Was that the first funeral you've been to?"

"What? No. I mean, others, when I was younger." She shrugged.

"Well," I said, also trying to keep my voice light. The sun had sunk lower in the sky, turning the perch gold and peach colored, giving everything an otherworldly glow. "When we're old and in a nursing home, we can write our wills together. *Cremation only. All money to go to an animal shelter.*" She snorted—it was essentially the will of one of her great-aunts, many years ago, who had caused a pretty big scandal in the family, Charlotte had told me. Her fifteen cats and dogs had been well-provided for: her children, not as much, though, Charlotte acceded, they had probably deserved it less.

"Right," Charlotte said. "Nursing home. Something to look forward to."

"It's better than the alternative."

"Death? Maybe." She considered, cocking her head, bright sunlight spilling across her pale face and dark curls, making her look like a painting come to life.

I should have asked then. Why death had been coming up so often. Why she was dwelling on it, what shadow had

crept over her. I was her best friend, and I did not see it—
or rather, did not want to. I just tried to cheer her up,
pretend that it was all going to be okay, because we were
young and terrible things like cremation and burial, they
could never happen to us.

They weren't supposed to.

CHAPTER 28

*A*iden's eyes met mine. I couldn't breathe.

Tell me, I thought, but another part of me wanted to silence him, to keep him from saying the words that meant that Charlotte was irrevocably lost, that I would never see her again.

I tried to read the answer in his eyes, but they were wild. He stood frozen just a step inside the café, lips pale, skin paler, damp hair curled against his ears. It was as though someone had whispered a spell, and we were both stuck there, frozen in time, in some suspended scene where Charlotte *could* be alive and *could* be dead, so like Schrödinger's cat she was actually both.

Riley stepped in front of me, blocking Aiden from my sight.

"What do you want, Aiden?" he said. Voice low, almost shaking. I saw the police officers look up, blandly interested. Behind me, Danny sank further into his seat.

"Who are you?" Aiden sneered, for a moment every bit

the affronted noble, forced to speak to someone well beneath his class. It had to be an act; surely he couldn't have forgotten Riley in so short a span of time.

I moved around Riley so that I could see them both. Aiden's gaze floated back to me; I still couldn't read anything in it. "Is—" I began, but I couldn't finish the question. My throat seized up. I began to feel faint and leaned on the chair beside me, taking in a long breath.

"Here, sit down," Aiden said gruffly, moving forward to pull one of the seats of the table out. It was the one in front of where I had been sitting with Danny; I had moved only three yards before collapsing. Great.

Aiden sat down at the table with me. Riley, ignoring both of our stares, took the final, third seat.

"Reese," Danny said behind me. His voice was high-pitched, frantic. "Reese, you said you'd tell them—"

"Shut up, Danny, not now," Riley snapped. Even Aiden gave him a surprised, sideways look at that.

"Riley, can you give us a minute?" I said. I would have suggested to Aiden we go outside, go somewhere private, but I wasn't sure I was able to stand. My legs were still shaking beneath the table. Who knew that grief, that *fear*, could be so physical?

"Sure," Riley said, "why don't the three of us go outside?"

"*You* go outside," Aiden said. "I'm here to talk to Reese."

Riley's jaw clenched; the police officers had moved a few feet closer now, and I wondered if they were trying to eavesdrop. As if any of us had anything incriminating to say. I glared at them, long and hard, but their gazes never lifted to mine. They were as casual and cool as ever, sharks circling the water, taking their time.

"Riley, *give us a minute*," I said. "Please."

He glanced at the door. "Okay," he said. "One minute. Then you'll both meet me outside? I have to tell you something."

"Both of us?" I said, momentarily distracted.

"Both of you."

Aiden frowned, but Riley had already stood and slid out the door, not even looking at the police officers.

My heart pounded in my chest. I closed my eyes for a moment, pressing the lids together. This, I thought, could be the very last moment that I know my best friend might be alive. This would be the moment I truly lost her.

Everything happened very quickly after that.

I heard motion behind me, a screeching sound, and then a body whipped past. In front of me, the cops moved just as fast, blocking the door with a quickness that belied their feigned casualness. Aiden shot up and moved in front of me, tensed, not sure where to go or what he was doing and caught in the same frenzy of movement that I was.

I had half-risen from my seat, legs still shaking, as Danny ricocheted off of Officer Stone. She threw out her arms to soften the blow, but the force of a young football player still knocked her off balance, and Officer Bordeaux caught her as her hip cracked into the table behind. Danny, face wild, arms flailing, righted himself and pushed for the door.

"Hey!" someone in the café yelled—barista?

Customer? It didn't matter. No one listened. Danny leapt the three steps onto the sidewalk and angled himself forward—only to be checked immediately by Riley's shoulder.

This time, it was Danny who went down. I had managed to straighten, but I still felt as though all of my movements were through syrup. Aiden was still positioned in front of me, arms half out, but the cops had recovered and pounded out the door, shouting and waving hands and whistles and cuffs—no, those weren't cuffs, my imagination was playing tricks on me—but they surrounded Danny and Riley and the two boys backed away, up against the café, Danny nursing a sore shoulder and looking, for all things, like he was about to cry.

I could see the wind whipping at their hair and eyes as they stood back. Riley exchanged a few quick words with the cops and moved off, leaving only Danny in front of them. The café patrons crowded close to see, blocking my view. Aiden, tall as he was, didn't even have to crane his neck: he kept his eyes trained on the glass, on the scene unfolding just outside.

Screw it, I thought. I stood up on my chair.

I had half-expected to see Danny with his hands cuffed behind his back, being marched off to some police cruiser where the police would place one hand on his head and gently guide it inside the car, lips moving as they recited his rights…but no, Officer Bordeaux was helping Danny up, and Danny was saying something to Officer Stone, head hung low, shoulders slumped forward as his feet staggered to find his center of weight again. Officer Bordeaux dusted off his shoulders and waved—friendly but menacing—at all the faces gathered at the window. The crowd inside the café collectively jumped, turning to pretend to be examining wall art or tidying up tables or grabbing a few extra packets of sweetener. They dispersed slowly, gazes still twitching over to the window. I climbed down off the chair, heart still pounding in my chest.

I searched for Riley, but he was nowhere to be found, not yet. I could feel my pulse like a drumbeat in my neck, roaring in my ears. My eyes slid sideways at Aiden, but his gaze was fastened on Danny, calculating. Had Danny done something after all? *They were dating,* I wanted to say, to read the reaction on his face. *Or something. She never told me. Why did she never tell me?*

Danny was gesticulating now at the cops. I tried to read something in his body language: anger? desperation? fear? Protest—that was all I could tell for sure. Officer Stone and Officer Bordeaux's expressions were hidden in the fading light, their bodies a blaze of orange, their faces in dark shadow. I thought that they had their hands clasped behind their backs. Non-threatening. *We're not about to arrest you.* Even if they were.

Were they?

Aiden stepped closer to me. I felt the warmth of him against my side, from my shoulder down to my hip. It felt protective somehow, electric. I tried not to breathe, wondering if the movement had been accidental, wondering why I cared, annoyed at my body for reacting even now, with everything going to pieces around me.

"They're taking him," Aiden said, a low rumble.

I froze. Indeed, in the deepening shadows of the evening, I could make out Officer Stone and Officer Bordeaux arranging themselves on either side of Danny. Still no cuffs. He walked with them, head down, folded in on himself, like a monster corralled by two hunters. It looked to me like they were about to walk through some portal, out of this world altogether. I had the crazy, intense urge to run after them, call for them to stop.

And what about Danny's request? Had I let him down, not telling the cops that I knew nothing of his and Charlotte's relationship? No, no, that couldn't matter; if something had been going on, and *something* had, it didn't matter whether I knew it or not. It didn't change the truth. I didn't have to cover for anyone. Not if—

I turned to Aiden. Braced myself. I saw him shift towards me, broad shoulders tilting my way, icy blue eyes meeting mine. He looked so much like her, in the warm light of the café. The same slanted nose, the same sharp cheekbones, the same wide eyes. Everything elven, ethereal.

"Tell me," I said.

He didn't have to ask. He knew exactly what I meant. "It's not her."

"What?"

"The body. It's not Charlotte. They still haven't found her."

This time I did collapse. Aiden caught me, which was embarrassing enough that my body jerked alert again, and I found my footing. "Sorry," I said, lowering myself into the seat. "Sorry, I—" My throat closed again. I began, ridiculously, to cry.

Aiden sat down next to me. Took my hand once more. When I looked up again, I saw the single tear making its diamond track down his cheek.

Charlotte, I thought, *where are you?*

The warm evening gave no answer.

CHAPTER 29

The DNA was not a match. That was what Aiden told me, when I was capable of having a conversation again. "Then who is it?" I had asked.

He shook his head. He didn't know. *A girl?* Yes. *A young girl?* Yes. *But not Charlotte?* No.

I hadn't realized how much I had expected it to be her until he told me. I felt like Charlotte had been resurrected, like the world had burst into a thousand colors in front of my eyes. Like some magical Pied Piper had blown a flute and summoned the ghosts of the world back to the land of the living—or something.

"Come on," Aiden said. I realized, with a start, how many eyes were on us: the spectacle outside was gone, and in the interim we had replaced it. I stood, and Aiden guided me out by the shoulders and into the dim evening. Our breath came out in spirals of white; I hunched down in my coat, letting myself be led by Aiden as he kept his light touch on my shoulders. A couple beeps and flashes of red light and we were at his car.

"Mine's over there," I said, sudden panic streaking through me, like it had a few weeks ago when Charlotte had suggested we escape somewhere, leave some party, and I had that flash of responsibility: *my car, I can't leave my car*.

"I'll drive you over," Aiden said.

I got in the passenger side. The heated seat was already on, and warm air began blowing at me as if the car had been holding its breath, a living thing waiting for its master to reappear. Aiden climbed in the other side and turned it on.

For a moment, that sense of danger sliced through me again—I was alone, at someone's mercy. And Charlotte was gone. My breathing quickened, and it was with an effort that I slowed it again. And anyway, Aiden pulled onto the street leading up to the stadium parking lot, driving at a slow twenty miles an hour. He turned on his blinker and pulled right. "Somewhere nearby?" he asked.

I gave him directions, and we wound our way around the now mostly empty lot, my pulse slowing as it became clear I had not suddenly jumped into some movie abduction scene. Aiden pulled to a stop, but didn't shut the engine. The heat continued to blast, almost too efficient. I turned the vents from me and Aiden cracked a window.

"Sorry," he said, fiddling with the dials.

It was time for me to get out now; I recognized that, but still I stayed immobile in the front seat, wanting to say so much but not knowing where to start. I wanted him to tell me again that the body had not been Charlotte's. That they were still looking.

"How are your parents?" I said instead.

He shrugged. "Fine."

"Did they think—Were they—?"

"Yeah," Aiden said. When he looked at me, his mouth was grim, eyes haunted. "Yeah, we all did."

I wanted to take his hand, but that was the kind of smoothness that only Charlotte could pull off, the kind of comfort that would have been natural and easy for her, and was awkward and jilted for me. And so I only muttered that I was sorry. "If I can do anything," I said, not bothering to explain that I was *already* doing something, that I was going to help find out what happened to Charlotte, come hell or high water.

He looked out the front windshield, bright red and white lights of the car sending shadows scurrying up his face. I would have left then and said my good-byes, but he had not yet said no. I felt him waiting to tell me something, all the unspoken words spooling at the back of his throat, within that clenched jaw.

I waited. Alone in a car with the brother of my missing best friend, the boy who, until this past week, I had never spent even a second alone with. He was so familiar to me, and yet such a stranger, too. I had no idea what words would spill out of his mouth—confession? Plea? Rebuff?

"Tell me," I said, when I couldn't take anymore.

Aiden twitched. "Tell you what?"

"Whatever you're thinking about. Debating. Just tell me; I can handle it."

He sized me up. "Yeah," he said. "You probably could. But some things aren't really for me to tell."

"Is it about Danny?"

A lip twisted back. Scorn. "What, the kid you were with? Of course not."

"Then what?"

For a moment, I thought he would say. He took a deep breath, his lean frame swelling with it, secrets inflating to life, ready to be spilled at the exhale. But then he shook his head again. "I can't really say—Charlotte was going through a tough time, these past couple of weeks. You probably noticed."

Had I? I thought back, to Charlotte's somewhat more eccentric recklessness, her disregard for school start times and the boundaries of lunch hour, her pressing need for us to do everything that senior year, experience everything, have last hurrahs everywhere. The change had been regular senioritis, I was sure of it. What else lurked beneath? What had I missed?

"Why?" I blurted out.

"She was a little down," Aiden said, which of course didn't answer my question. "I just hope…it can't have had anything to do with…" He cut off abruptly, and it was only a minute later, when I raised my eyes to his, that I saw why. He looked like he was trying very hard not to cry.

"We'll find her," I said. This time I did pat his arm, awkwardly, because it seemed almost worse not to. "It'll be okay. We'll find her, I promise."

When he looked at me, it was with a mixture of hope and disdain, the strong desire to believe what I was saying and the equally strong desire to scorn it, to call me out on making promises that I didn't know I could keep.

"She always said how smart you were," Aiden said. It broke my heart to hear the desperate wish there. "That you saw things nobody else did, especially here. In St. Clair."

"She did?" I didn't care that it sounded like I was

digging for compliments. I wanted any little nugget of Charlotte I could get, now that she was gone. Every little crumb.

"Yeah. That you were the last real girl around here, whatever that meant." He laughed, shakily, and glanced over at me. My stomach jumped. I was aware, suddenly, of how close I was to Aiden Walters, with his crystal blue eyes glistening with tears, his long limbs nearly touching mine, his face turned towards me, searching for something.

I thought, *he would kiss me right now, if I leaned forward.*

It would have been a lie to say that I had never thought of kissing Aiden Walters. He was Charlotte's brother, omnipresent, and he was good-looking in that sharp and untouchable way that made him all the more safe to dream about, because those dreams had such a sense of unreality. But never had I actually considered flirting with him, or making any kind of move on him. He was Charlotte's brother, Charlotte's territory.

And yet, he was one of the only people feeling the intensity of the pain that I was now. One of the only people who truly knew the heartache I was going through. I felt a dizzy sense that if we kissed, our pain would meld together, be sucked from our bodies and consumed by something else, something more powerful, and more dangerous.

Not like this.

The words popped into my head just as, I thought, Aiden leaned a fraction forward. I couldn't be sure—it might all have been in my head, the intensity of his look, the leaning—but I turned my shoulder and fiddled with my purse.

"Keep me updated," I said, holding up my cell phone, as if that even required explanation. "Don't worry. We'll find her."

Aiden's face had gone stoic again. "Right," he said. "Yes. Thanks, Reese. Oh, and Reese?"

"Yes?"

"I'm sorry. About earlier. I know you didn't have anything to do with it—I was just angry. Stressed."

"I know. I understand."

He waited until I walked to my car and had gotten safely in. I waved to him, though I wasn't sure if he could see it in the deepening night—*See? All safe.*—and then he roared off, engine snarling, and I was alone.

I WAS JUST PULLING out of the parking lot when I saw Riley, head ducked down, hands shoved into his pockets. I stopped, and he shielded his eyes from my headlights to try and make me out, freezing up like a prey animal.

"It's me," I said.

"Reese?"

"Yeah."

He relaxed.

"Do you need a ride?" I offered.

"No, car is in here. Hey, safe trip back home, okay?"

"Wait," I said, as he began to move off. "What was so important? That you had to tell me?"

He blinked up at the bright lights, expression shifting, hard to read in the darkness. "Nothing," he said finally, voice low, a little defiant, a little apologetic. "It's just—nothing, right now."

"Okay." The cold air was swooshing into my car, beating back the heat from the feeble vents. I shivered and rubbed my hands on my thighs. "Nothing? You sure?" *You said it was important*, I wanted to remind him. *You made it sound like it was urgent. Like I had to follow you right then. What changed?*

"Sorry," Riley said. "It was—I got a little worked up. It's nothing."

Liar, I thought. But I rolled my window up, let Riley rush across the front of my car and into the lot to find his own. It didn't matter, though. Whatever secrets he was trying to hide, I'd find them out. I'd never been more sure of anything.

CHAPTER 30

*W*hen I got home, I turned on the stove to heat some milk for a decaf chai tea. I made it the way that my mother made it, huge dark star anises and cinnamon sticks, luxuries to contrast with the sad little scrunched tea bags that we also used, since it was cheaper at the grocery store than loose leaf. I poured a healthy dollop of honey in and watched the cream froth and bubble, thinking of when Charlotte had last been over, of when we had made this together.

It had been a week ago. Her car was in the shop, so my mother had picked us up, offered to take us up the long and winding road to the Walters'. I hesitated. Then I asked, "Can Charlotte come study at our place?"

My mother had blinked back at me in the rearview mirror. Charlotte hardly ever came over, by my choice. I didn't invite her. Our small little townhouse was nothing compared to her mansion. My mother worked all the time, and we couldn't afford cleaners, and I was less helpful than I liked to admit. Our house seemed to collect clutter, a fact

I had only really noticed as I had gotten older, as I had seen houses like Charlotte's that were pristine, open, everything in its proper place.

But Charlotte had told me that day that she hadn't wanted to go home, not yet. And so I asked.

"Well, I haven't had time to tidy up," my mother said. Her perennial line, when we were about to have someone over. "Charlotte, you sure you don't want me to take you home? It's no trouble."

"No, Mrs. E., if that's all right—my dad can pick me up later after work."

And so we had ended up in the kitchen, and my mom had suggested chai tea, and Charlotte had acted excited even though I was embarrassed to bring out the teabags, to show her that we bootlegged something authentic.

She didn't see it that way, though. "Wow," she had said, watching me stir. "Can I try? So you guys take these and really, like, fancy them up." She pointed to the teabags before taking the spoon from me. "This smells *amazing*."

I thought of her there in my kitchen as I stirred the tea now. Even then, she must have been seeing Danny. Even then, she must have been sad, depressed, down, for reasons which Aiden couldn't or wouldn't explain. Even then, whatever had happened to her had been in the works, dark shadows creeping at the edges of her, waiting to swallow her whole.

But in my memory it was just Charlotte, stirring, smiling, delighted with the ritual because it was new, because she was my friend.

"You should seriously sell this," Charlotte said, as we poured the mixture into two clay mugs, the misshapen ones that I had made in elementary school, one of them with something that was supposed to be an elephant trunk on the front that had long since snapped off. "This is so good. You always keep those spices?"

"Yeah, my mom's really into them."

She blew on the top of her mug, large eyes on mine. I thought of her now, even as I shut the stove off and, carefully, poured some of the newly brewed mixture into that same old clay mug. I poured another measure out for my mother, for when she had finished showering, and went to sit at the counter stool, imagining Charlotte was still there, imagining I was face-to-face with her, that I could ask her anything. In my mind her long legs were swinging, her elbows on the counter, her face lit up from above with the ceiling lights and below from the three candles my mother always had burning on the counter, when she was home. Pine and peppermint candles. The same ones that I had going now.

"Where did you go?" I whispered, and in my mind Charlotte turned to look at me, lips pressed into a smile. She had a secret, and she wouldn't tell me. Or she couldn't, not now, not where she had gone. I saw her sweep her long dark hair back from her face, sigh, blow at the chai tea as one finger traced the pattern of the counter. "Charlotte."

The eyes returned to me. I knew I was imagining it all, imagining it with the force of a conjuring. Charlotte wasn't really there, but I still saw her in my mind's eye, those eyes snapping up to mine, something in them suddenly alert, electric.

"Tell me where you are," I said. "Tell me how to help you."

Eyes widened. Her lips moved, but I couldn't hear anything. My heart thudded in my chest. I set my mug down.

"The lake."

I swear I heard it, faint as a whisper, probably just the wind whipping through the house, probably my own imagination pulling it from my subconscience. But the words held fast there, even as the apparition faded away, and I was left alone in my kitchen, pulse racing, the scent of spices and pine suddenly hot and fierce in my nostrils.

I took a deep breath, sighed. Shut my eyes.

Charlotte was still out there somewhere.

And I was going to find her.

ALSO BY L.C. WARMAN

The Disappearance of Charlotte Walters

The Last Real Girl

The Last Real Crime

The Last Real Secret

AFTERWORD

Thank you for reading! To stay up-to-date on L.C. Warman's new releases, subscribe to Greenleaf & Plympton's newsletter.

Greenleaf & Plympton is a boutique publisher of gothic novels, both modern and classic.

By "gothic," we specifically mean books of murder,

mystery, and magic. These books include some or all of the following characteristics:

- A mystery
- A tinge of the supernatural, a hint of magic, or just some sense that there is something more out there
- A sense of nostalgia, or of the past haunting the present
- A deep focus on character
- A style that is literary, but still accessible

These gothic books are NOT necessarily dark and dreary. They often couple a spooky atmosphere with cutting humor, or a sense of whimsy. They're not overly gory or violent, even though they may involve murder, disappearances, and battles.

Some of the recurring themes you might find in these books include:

- Old estates
- Family secrets
- Secret societies
- Criminal underworlds/black markets
- Blackmail
- Murder mysteries
- Trains, clocks, maps, and more
- Isolated hotels
- Old universities
- Mysterious figures

- Mistaken identities
- Circuses and magic shows
- Fortune-telling
- etc.

Are you just as big a fan of these books as us? Sign up to join our community of gothic book lovers, where we share exclusive stories, send letters both print and digital, and give you a gift on your birthday.

You can also browse our catalog of available gothic books at https://www.greenleafandplympton.com.

Welcome! We're so glad you found us.

ALSO AVAILABLE FROM GREENLEAF
& PLYMPTON

Classics

Jane Eyre
by Charlotte Brontë

The Count of Monte Cristo
by Alexandre Dumas

The Hound of the Baskervilles
by Sir Arthur Conan Doyle

The Turn of the Screw
by Henry James

Northanger Abbey
by Jane Austen

All of our classic titles are available in ebook and cloth hardcover, and can be embossed with a stamp of the reader's initials in gold foil. Shop on our site by visiting https://greenleafandplympton.com.

Modern Works

The Disappearance of Charlotte Walters
by L.C. Warman
The Last Real Girl (Book 1)
The Last Real Crime (Book 2)
The Last Real Secret (Book 3)

All of our modern titles are available in ebook and paperback. Find our full list of available titles by visiting https://greenleafandplympton.com.

Website: *https://greenleafandplympton.com*

instagram.com/greenleafandplympton

ABOUT THE AUTHOR

L.C. Warman is the author of spooky young adult mysteries. She grew up in New England, in a town where real estate contracts stipulated that you couldn't back out if you discovered your new place was haunted. She currently lives in a Michigan lakeside town with her husband and two dogs.

31213492

WITHDRAWN

DATE DUE

AUG 27 2024	

BRODART, CO.   Cat. No. 23-221

CPSIA information can be obtained
at www.ICGtesting.com
Printed in the USA
LVHW050735100619
620692LV00001B/50

Poestenkill Library

3 8125 10033 6826